BANK STREET COLLEGE PROJECT IN SCIENCE AND MATHEMATICS

THE VOYAGE OF THE MIMI

THE BOOK

The Bank Street College Project in Science and Mathematics
Samuel Y. Gibbon, Jr.—Executive Director

Based on the television series, "The Voyage of the *Mimi*" by

Richard M. Hendrick
Head Writer

John Griesemer

Paula Cizmar and Douglas Gower

Dramatic episodes adapted from the TV series by
Seymour Reit

Expeditions adapted from the TV series by
Mary Fitzpatrick

Activities for the dramatic episodes written by
Ellen Schecter

Activities for the expeditions written by
Eileen Mitchell

Editor
Lorin Driggs

WINGS
for learning

1600 Green Hills Road
P.O. Box 660002
Scotts Valley, CA 95067
(800) 321-7511 • (408) 438-5502

CONTENTS

THE MIMI

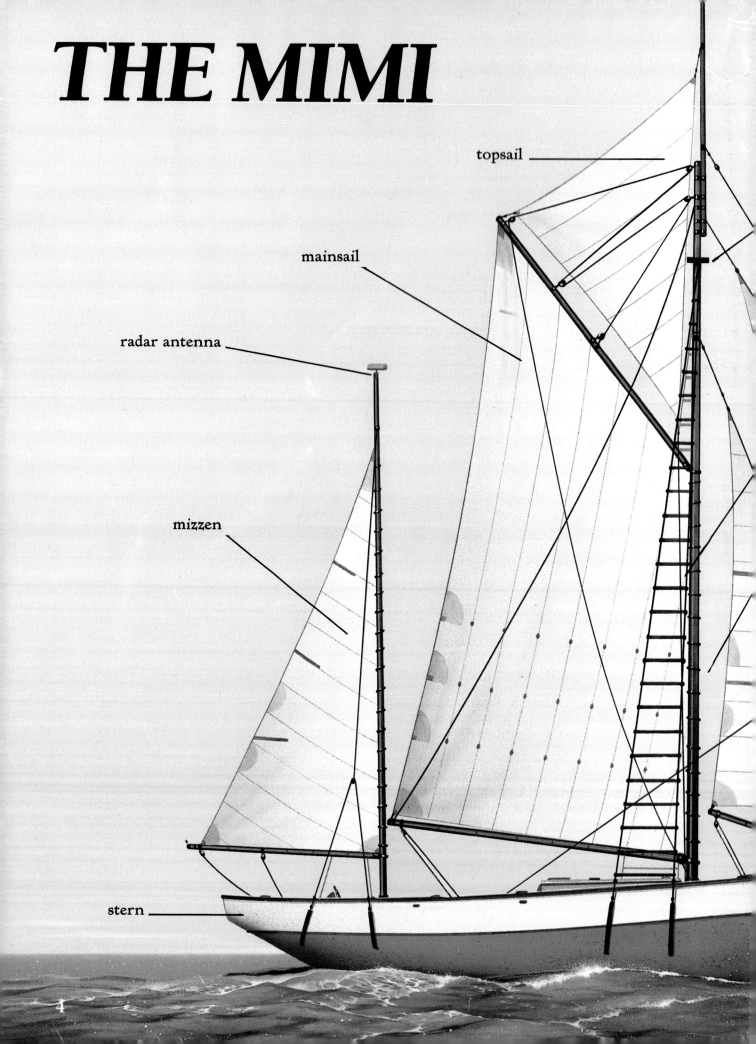

topsail

mainsail

radar antenna

mizzen

stern

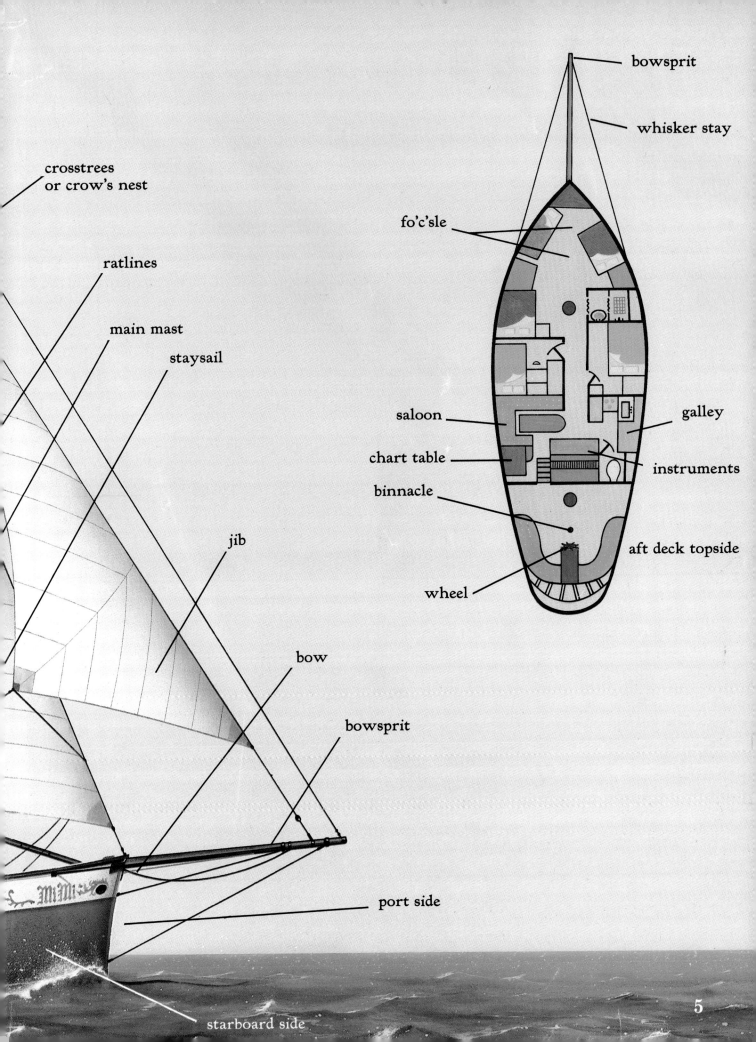

crosstrees
or crow's nest

ratlines

main mast

staysail

jib

bow

bowsprit

port side

starboard side

bowsprit

whisker stay

fo'c'sle

saloon

galley

chart table

instruments

binnacle

aft deck topside

wheel

5

HUMPBACK WHALE

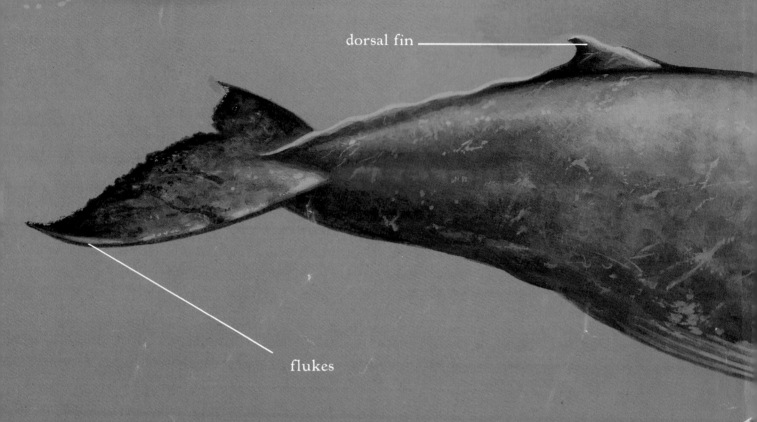

dorsal fin

flukes

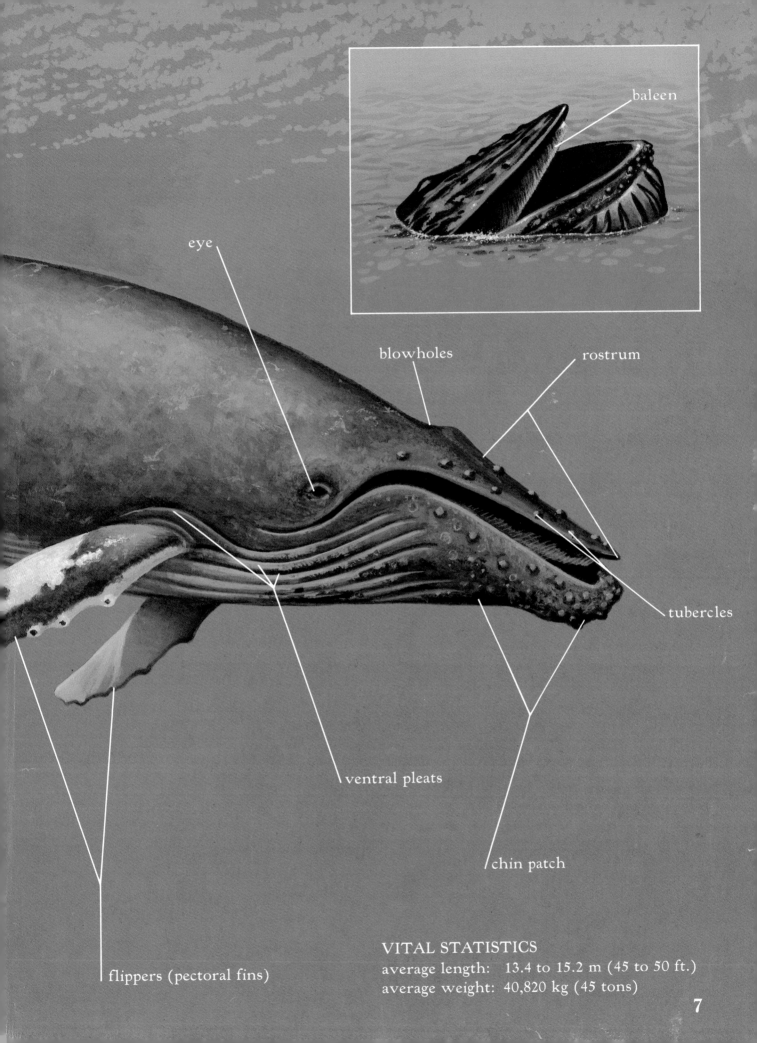

baleen

eye

blowholes

rostrum

tubercles

ventral pleats

chin patch

flippers (pectoral fins)

VITAL STATISTICS
average length: 13.4 to 15.2 m (45 to 50 ft.)
average weight: 40,820 kg (45 tons)

7

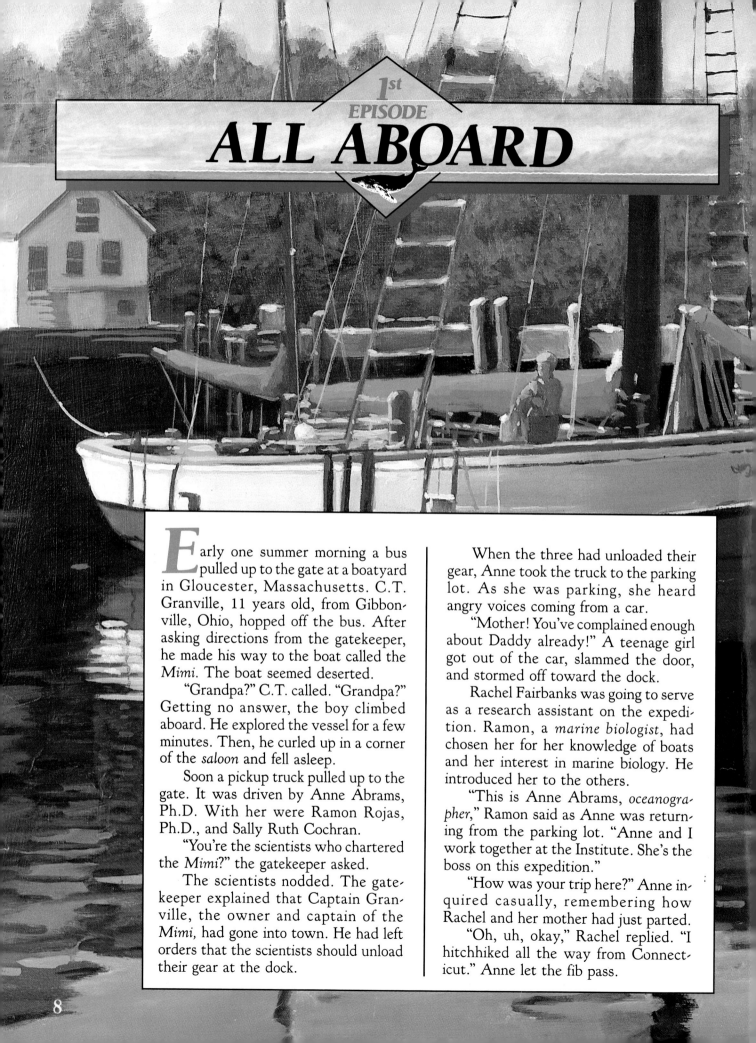

ALL ABOARD

Early one summer morning a bus pulled up to the gate at a boatyard in Gloucester, Massachusetts. C.T. Granville, 11 years old, from Gibbonville, Ohio, hopped off the bus. After asking directions from the gatekeeper, he made his way to the boat called the *Mimi*. The boat seemed deserted.

"Grandpa?" C.T. called. "Grandpa?" Getting no answer, the boy climbed aboard. He explored the vessel for a few minutes. Then, he curled up in a corner of the *saloon* and fell asleep.

Soon a pickup truck pulled up to the gate. It was driven by Anne Abrams, Ph.D. With her were Ramon Rojas, Ph.D., and Sally Ruth Cochran.

"You're the scientists who chartered the *Mimi*?" the gatekeeper asked.

The scientists nodded. The gatekeeper explained that Captain Granville, the owner and captain of the *Mimi,* had gone into town. He had left orders that the scientists should unload their gear at the dock.

When the three had unloaded their gear, Anne took the truck to the parking lot. As she was parking, she heard angry voices coming from a car.

"Mother! You've complained enough about Daddy already!" A teenage girl got out of the car, slammed the door, and stormed off toward the dock.

Rachel Fairbanks was going to serve as a research assistant on the expedition. Ramon, a *marine biologist*, had chosen her for her knowledge of boats and her interest in marine biology. He introduced her to the others.

"This is Anne Abrams, *oceanographer*," Ramon said as Anne was returning from the parking lot. "Anne and I work together at the Institute. She's the boss on this expedition."

"How was your trip here?" Anne inquired casually, remembering how Rachel and her mother had just parted.

"Oh, uh, okay," Rachel replied. "I hitchhiked all the way from Connecticut." Anne let the fib pass.

"And this is Sally Ruth Cochran, our senior research assistant," Ramon continued. "She's a senior in college, majoring in marine biology."

Rachel smiled and turned to look at the *Mimi.* "Well, it floats," she quipped, "but can it move?"

"It was built for work, not for speed," Sally Ruth explained.

Rachel saw that Sally Ruth used sign language when she spoke. "Is she . . . deaf?" Rachel asked Ramon.

But Sally Ruth answered. "Yes, I am deaf, but I can read lips."

Rachel smiled awkwardly and said to Ramon, "Are we the whole crew?"

"No. There's one more to come."

Just then Captain Granville came stomping along the dock. He'd been waiting in vain at the bus station, and was not in a good mood.

"Any of you see a young boy around here?" he barked. "My grandson. He must have taken the wrong bus."

"What does he look like?" Rachel asked.

"Don't know," snapped the Captain. "Haven't seen him in eight years. Get your gear on board," he told the group. "I hope he turns up on the next bus."

In the cabin below, C.T. was awakened by all the noise. When he opened his eyes his grandfather was standing over him.

"You C.T. Granville?" the Captain demanded.

"Yes, sir," C.T. answered.

"You always put people out of sorts?" the Captain asked. "You put me out of sorts. I was all over that bus station looking for you."

C.T. explained, "The bus driver let me out here. I told him about your boat."

At that, the Captain softened a little bit. "How are things at home?" he asked.

"Ma's okay, but she still has to stay in bed until she has the baby."

"I know," Captain Granville said. "That's why you're here – so you'll be out of her hair."

A few minutes later, the Captain introduced C.T. and announced, "He'll be sailing with us."

Anne was surprised. She hadn't planned on another person. She wondered if there would be room.

"We can squeeze him into the *fo'c'sle*," Ramon suggested.

The Captain added, "That's what I was figuring to do."

"Well . . . okay," she said. "Let's get to work."

When the equipment and gear were aboard the *Mimi*, Captain Granville gave his crew a tour of the quarters. Space was cramped. The shower room would have to double as the darkroom where Sally Ruth could develop her photographs.

Everyone got to work stowing the gear. On deck, the Captain handed C.T. a marking pen and pointed to some cans.

"Write on the tops of the cans what's in them," he said. "If they get wet and the paper soaks off, they won't have labels. Then we won't know our canned peas from our fruit cocktail."

Rachel talked with Ramon as he was putting away his books. "Why does Sally Ruth use sign language when she can talk?" she asked.

"So we can all learn how to sign."

Later, on deck, the Captain called to Sally Ruth, who was working with her back toward him. "Miss, please hand me that hammer. Miss! MISS!"

Then he walked over and spoke angrily to her. Reading his lips and the expression on his face, Sally Ruth said, "It doesn't help to shout. I'm deaf."

Furious, the Captain confronted Anne. "Miss Abrams, you told me you hired an experienced crew. Then you bring a deaf mute on board!"

"She's not mute," Ramon said as he emerged from the galley.

"Captain Granville," Anne said, "Sally Ruth practically grew up on a boat. What does her being deaf matter? You can get her attention. Watch."

Anne took the Captain's hammer and tapped it against the railing on

which Sally Ruth's hand rested. Feeling the vibrations, Sally Ruth immediately looked up from her work. Captain Granville reluctantly concluded that he didn't have to worry about Sally Ruth's deafness.

Later, in the saloon, C.T. learned that the scientists had chartered the *Mimi* to study humpback whales.

"Wow!" he exclaimed. "I've never seen a whale. I'd never even seen the ocean until today."

Suddenly, the sound of blaring rock music filled the cabin. Anne smiled knowingly and rushed up on deck.

Arthur Spencer was hurrying along the dock carrying a large radio. Anne had chosen Arthur, a high school student from the Bronx in New York City, to be the other research assistant on the expedition. He knew a lot about electronics, especially computers.

"Arthur!" Anne called to him. "Sorry I'm late, Doc," he said over the din. "We had a flat tire on the turnpike."

"Arthur, this may not be the best place to play your box," Anne said. "Our captain's a little touchy."

"Oh, that's cool," he said, holding up a pair of earphones. "I'm wired for silence, too."

Below deck, Anne introduced Arthur to Ramon, Sally Ruth, and Rachel. In the fo'c'sle, he met C.T. and learned that they would be bunkmates.

"Some boat! Who's the driver?" Arthur asked.

Just then, Captain Granville came by and saw the radio.

"What's that?" he asked Arthur.

"Uh, briefcase," Arthur said, intimidated by the Captain's gruffness.

"Stow it!" the Captain ordered.

"Who was that?" Arthur asked.

"Uh, that's my grandfather. He's also the driver," C.T. said.

"That dude's a grandfather?"

Suddenly, the *Mimi*'s engines roared to life. "All hands on deck! Let's go!" the Captain called. "On the double!"

The crew scrambled to the deck as the boat pulled away from the dock. The voyage of the *Mimi* was under way.

Sea Lingo

Imagine you've just stepped aboard the *Mimi* for your maiden voyage. You've got your sea legs, and you're ready to do your part as a member of the crew. But you don't know what to do because you can't understand what the people are saying.

Read what each crew member is saying. Decide if sentence *a* or *b* is the right translation. Compare your translation with your classmates'. Can you think of other possible translations?

"All hands on deck! On the double!"
a. "Hold your cards above the table. All bets double or nothing."
b. "Everybody come up on deck right away."

"Whales breaching off the port bow!"
a. "Whales are jumping out of the water on the left-hand side of the boat."
b. "Whales are breaking the part of the boat where the wine is stored."

"The Captain is aft."
a. "The Captain can't hear very well."
b. "The Captain is at the rear of the boat."

"Stow all the grub in the galley."
a. "Store all the food in the boat's kitchen."
b. "Donate all your worms to the art museum."

"Ahoy, mates! Let's make sail!"
a. "Oh, boy! Husbands and wives, bring cloth, needles, and thread so we can sew some sails."
b. "Hey, everybody! Let's put up the sails and get moving!"

Handmade Words

Would you like to learn to "speak" without making a sound? Learning the "hand-made" American Sign Language alphabet is the first step. Use the alphabet to finger-spell words letter by letter. You can learn American Sign Language just the way you learn any other language. And keep your eye on Sally Ruth and Anne throughout "The Voyage of the *Mimi*."

American Sign Language has special signs for whole words, phrases, and sentences. When you put all this "hand talk" together, you can say anything in the world! Start by learning to finger-spell your name.

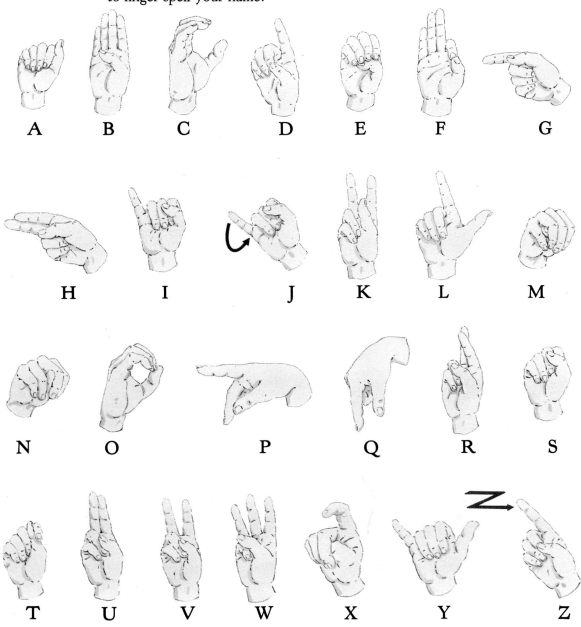

A   B   C   D   E   F   G

H   I   J   K   L   M

N   O   P   Q   R   S

T   U   V   W   X   Y   Z

The story of "The Voyage of the *Mimi*" is made up, but the events in it really could happen. There are scientists who go out to sea to study whales. In fact, scientists travel just about everywhere to study just about everything. The actors who play C.T. Granville, Arthur Spencer, and Rachel Fairbanks travel too. After each episode in "The Voyage of the *Mimi*," one of them visits a place where people are doing interesting scientific work.

Ben Affleck is the actor who plays the role of C.T. Ben is 11 years old, just like C.T., and he lives in Cambridge, Massachusetts. Many months after "The Voyage of the *Mimi*" was filmed, Ben went to Boston, Massachusetts, to visit the New England Aquarium with Dr. Sylvia Earle. The Aquarium is a good place to learn about the oceans, especially if you're with Dr. Earle. She's a marine biologist and deep sea diver.

"Where there is water, there is life," claims Dr. Earle, "and the ocean is absolutely filled with life. Life on the earth started out in the ocean before *evolution* brought some species on to land, and 90 percent of life on the planet is still to be found in the oceans.

"If you came from outer space and wanted to understand this planet, it would be a good idea to look first in the oceans. In fact, because of the photos that astronauts have brought back to us from outer space, we have begun to appreciate the watery nature of our planet. From out there, the earth looks mainly blue and white because oceans cover 70 percent of our planet. Only in the last 20 years or so have we begun to realize the major ways that water affects our lives.

"Climate, weather, temperature, rainfall, oxygen—all these things that we take for granted come from and are controlled by the ocean. It's amazing that we have explored hundreds of thousands of miles out into space, but have explored so little of the oceans.

"People tend to think of the oceans as limitless. They throw things in the water and think, 'out of sight, out of mind.' Of course, this is not true. Imagine what it would be like if a flock of creatures constantly flew overhead dropping trash on us. That's what we do to the fish. For them, the sea is a total environment—their air, their food, and the atmosphere that touches their bodies are all the same thing. When we dump trash or chemicals into the sea, bits of minerals or trace elements from these waste materials are enough to alter the environment for the fish and other creatures that live there. And whatever changes or harms the oceans could eventually change or harm us in some way. I think we abuse the environment through neglect rather than as an evil intent. Now that we are becoming aware of the effects of our actions, it is time to change. I'm certain that it's not too late for us to live in harmony with the sea."

Sylvia has been interested in the sea and its creatures since she was a girl growing up in Florida, with the Gulf of Mexico as her backyard. Not only has she studied the creatures of the sea, she has joined them in their environment. In a number of experimental ocean dives, Dr. Earle has relied on diving suits and underwater vehicles that recreate the air and pressure conditions found on land.

In one dive, Sylvia tested out a new diving suit

that looks like a giant space suit. On land this suit weighs 1,000 pounds, but in the water it weighs only 60 pounds. Not connected by a lifeline to the surface, Dr. Earle was able to make the deepest free dive that anyone has ever made. She walked around at a depth of 1,250 feet for 2½ hours.

As part of another experiment called *Tektite II*, Sylvia lived for two weeks in an underwater laboratory in the Caribbean Sea with a group of other scientists. They could leave their laboratory through a hole in the floor, and go out and swim with the fish. "It was like having your own private swimming pool, but without any sides to it," said Sylvia.

Dr. Earle has taken part in half a dozen such experiments in underwater living, and has been deep sea diving hundreds of times. She says that she knows there are some people who just don't like to get wet. Still she finds it odd that all people haven't put their faces in the ocean to see what the fish are doing. "There are so many wonderful things down there, I don't know why people aren't just jumping into the water all over the place!"

One reason that people can't just jump into the water all over the place is the amount of equipment they need in order to survive in the deep sea. However, whales and dolphins—which are mammals like us—are adapted beautifully to the marine environment. There is nothing on their bodies to make their progress through the water slow or difficult. Their bodies are sleek and streamlined, and their skin is smooth and nearly hairless. To maintain their body heat in cold water, whales and dolphins have a thick layer of blubber. Human beings must wear protective suits. Whales and dolphins breathe through blowholes in the tops of their heads, and barely have to break the water surface to breathe in and out. Human deep sea divers must carry a supply of air with them. And the flat tails of whales and dolphins propel them swiftly through the water. Human divers have to wear swim fins, or flippers, to get the same result.

The New England Aquarium has 70 tanks of fish. The tanks contain 2,500 fish from all over the world. Sylvia and Ben are looking at tropical reef fish.

During their visit to the Aquarium, Ben and Sylvia watched the sea lion and dolphin show. Sue Sinclair, the trainer of these performing sea mammals, is a friend of Sylvia's. After the show, Ben got to meet Sue and one of the dolphins named Sandy. He is a bottlenose dolphin who was captive-born. Sue explained that bottlenose dolphins do well in an aquarium environment because, in the wild, they live in waters close to shore. This means that they are accustomed to shallow water and are able to maneuver easily. It is clear that Sandy and Sue have a special relationship and that Sandy is quite smart. Sue said that Sandy learned his show behaviors faster than other show animals have.

Sylvia thought it would be nice for human divers to have some of Sandy's features and talents. "It is only by putting on all my equipment and getting into the water that I can have the lovely feeling of weightlessness that Sandy has all the time. Swimming is almost like flying, and swimming with dolphins is glorious," she said, "because they're so at ease with humans."

By the time Ben left the New England Aquarium, he felt he knew a lot more about the ocean. He appreciated how important it is in our lives, and he wished he could explore it as easily as whales and dolphins can.

The waves thudding on a distant shore are the heartbeat of man's ancestral home. The salt solution of the sea flows in man's veins, and—is it coincidence or part of nature's plan?—70 percent of man's body is water, the same proportion as the surface of the earth.

– Jacques-Yves Cousteau

I thought I would sail about a little and see the watery part of the world. Whenever I find myself growing grim about the mouth . . . I account it high time to get to sea as soon as I can. There is nothing surprising in this . . . Almost all men . . . some time or other, cherish very nearly the same feelings toward the ocean . . . They must get just as nigh the water as they possibly can without falling in.

– Herman Melville, Moby Dick

Sandy, a four-year-old bottlenose dolphin, is being fed by his trainer, Sue Sinclair. Not yet full grown, Sandy weighs 350 pounds, is 7½ feet long, and has 88 sharp teeth.

Approximately 21 million pounds of fish are landed each year at the Boston fishing pier. The oceans are a major food source for us. Overfishing is a problem, and quotas have been set on some kinds of fish to protect their populations.

Sandy, Carol, and Dixie are the stars of the dolphin show at the New England Aquarium.

SETTING SAIL

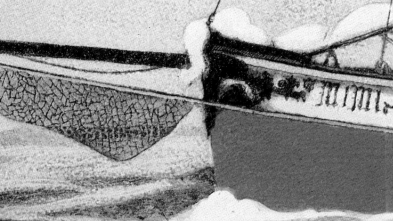

As the *Mimi* motored out of the harbor, C.T. tried to make conversation with his grandfather. . . without much luck.

"Are we going to see whales today, Grandpa?"

"You'll have to ask Dr. Abrams," replied the Captain gruffly.

"You mean Anne?" C.T. asked. Catching his grandfather's stern look, he added, "She said I could call her that."

But Captain Granville had no more time for conversation. "All hands! Let's make sail!" he called out. "Ramon, you and Dr. Abrams take the stops off the *mizzen* and take it up. You, uh, Arthur! You and Rebecca handle the *staysail halyard*. On the double!"

"What? Staysail? Halyard?" To Arthur, this sounded like a new language.

Rachel shouted back to the Captain, "It's not Rebecca! It's RACHEL! C'mon," she said to Arthur, showing him what they were supposed to do.

"Put your backs into it, you two! *Belay* that halyard! Raquel, get the furling line off the mainsail!"

Rachel couldn't believe he'd gotten her name wrong again. "That's Rachel!" She bounded onto the cabin top, leaving a bewildered Arthur to tie off the staysail halyard.

More orders from the Captain: "Keep an eye on those parrel beads, Rachel!"

Rachel shouted back in exasperation, "The name's Rach . . . Oh. Right!"

Meanwhile, Arthur's first attempt at tying off a line failed. The rope was coming undone. And just as the mainsail moved into place . . . the staysail dropped like a wounded bird.

"Don't just stand there!" the Captain barked. "Get it back up! And next time, Rachel, tie the line right!"

Rachel just about flipped. "Wait a minute, I didn't . . ."

But Captain Granville wasn't listening. "Let's go!" he shouted.

At last the *Mimi* cut the water under full sail. Everyone but Rachel and Captain Granville cheered.

"Yeah, terrific," snorted Rachel. "It only took us an hour to get five lousy sails up."

"Amen," agreed Captain Granville.

But Arthur was really getting into it. "What happens now?"

They all turned to the Captain for his answer. "Lunch."

In the *galley*, C.T. and Sally Ruth made sandwiches. When C.T. saw the peanut butter, he was staggered—a 25-pound jug! "This'll last a year!"

On deck, Rachel gave Arthur some sailing pointers. He was impressed by her skill.

"So your parents have a boat?" he asked.

"**They** don't have anything. They're separated. My father has an ocean racer. I crew for him."

"A boat like this one?"

"Arthur, a racing *sloop* is like a sportscar. This thing's a truck!"

They both laughed—and made sure Captain Granville hadn't heard.

Lunch gave the kids their first chance to get to know each other. Everyone was interested in Sally Ruth. As they ate their sandwiches, they learned she went to a college where all the students are deaf. They also learned from her that deaf people can have some unusual problems.

"It's hard to read your lips through the peanut butter," Sally Ruth laughed.

C.T. stayed on deck when the rest were called below for a meeting.

Anne and Ramon thought they might see whales soon because they were approaching Stellwagen Bank. It would be important that everyone know the goals of the mission. Anne reminded them. "We'll be observing

20

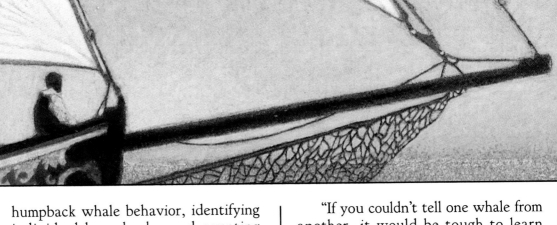

humpback whale behavior, identifying individual humpbacks, and counting them. And we'll be studying their *environment* by taking water temperatures and depth measurements."

Rachel joked, "Is that all?"

Ramon was an expert on humpbacks. "They are just returning from their winter mating grounds in the Caribbean. They haven't eaten much for four months, and they are HUN-GREE!"

He pointed to a chart of all kinds of whales. "You can tell if a whale is a humpback by its long white flippers, its bumpy head and chin, the shape of its *dorsal fin*, and by the black and white pattern on its tail."

Sally Ruth reminded Ramon that whales might be near and she went up to the *crow's nest* to be the lookout.

"If you couldn't tell one whale from another, it would be tough to learn anything about their movements and their habits," Anne pointed out.

Rachel was skeptical. "Can you really tell one whale from another?"

Ramon nodded. "You do it by looking at a part of the tail called the *flukes*. The pattern on the underside of a whale's flukes is like a fingerprint—different for every whale. If you get a good photograph of the fluke pattern, you can compare it to this catalogue of fluke photos. If you get a match, you can identify your whale."

Arthur looked through the book. "They each have an ID number."

"Yep. And some have names."

Just then C.T. stuck his head down the *companionway.* "Sally Ruth says there are whales two miles ahead!"

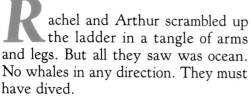**R**achel and Arthur scrambled up the ladder in a tangle of arms and legs. But all they saw was ocean. No whales in any direction. They must have dived.

C.T. looked out impatiently. "How long do they stay under?" he asked Anne.

"Five or ten minutes—even more."

Suddenly, 50 meters off *Mimi's bow*, a humpback whale leaped into the air and crashed down on its back on the ocean surface!

Arthur and Rachel were so excited they almost forgot that they were there to study, not just sightsee. But Ramon and Anne reminded them. "That was what we call a *breach*," Ramon said.

"We don't know why they do it, but we've seen them breach as many as fifty times in a row," Anne added.

"There are at least three adults, maybe five," Ramon noted. "It's hard to tell."

The whales were so awesome that C.T. forgot all about feeling uneasy with his grandfather. When another whale breached, he called out, "Hey, Grandpa! Look at that one!"

Anne and Rachel called out observations — behaviors and markings — to Arthur, who was trying to keep an accurate record. It wasn't easy when things were happening so fast. "What if I get behind?" Arthur wanted to know.

Ramon laughed. "We'll throw you overboard!"

A couple of whales started *lobtailing*. With their bodies straight down in the water and only their flukes showing, they slapped their tails down on the ocean surface repeatedly.

Rachel was a little concerned. "Are they mad at us?"

Anne didn't think so. "We've seen them do this from a long way off, so it isn't necessarily because of us. The fact is, we don't know why they lobtail."

No matter why, it was a great opportunity to see and photograph the undersides of their flukes, and Ramon took advantage of it. He thought he recognized one of the whales. "We'll know when the film's developed," he announced.

The crew watched the whales for the rest of the afternoon, recording behaviors and taking pictures. Only the setting of the sun stopped their work.

23

Later, Sally Ruth developed the day's photographs. She showed them to the other members of the crew.

Ramon was happy to see that one of his photos was indeed of a whale he knew from other voyages. When Anne suggested that the crew practice matching the photo to the catalogue photos, Ramon made a contest out of it.

"First one to match the photo with the correct fluke shot in the catalogue . . ."

". . . gets out of doing dishes for a week!" ventured Arthur.

"It's a deal!"

Jostling and nudging each other, the kids tore through the catalogue. C.T. thought he spotted the match. "Here it is! 0159!" But Arthur and Rachel paid no attention. They'd decided that all the patterns looked the same.

"There are over a thousand of those things," moaned Arthur.

Rachel thought they'd been fooled. "Nice trick, Ramon."

In the meantime, Anne had taken another copy of the photograph and was working with it at the computer. The computer screen now caught Arthur's attention. "Hey, what's that?"

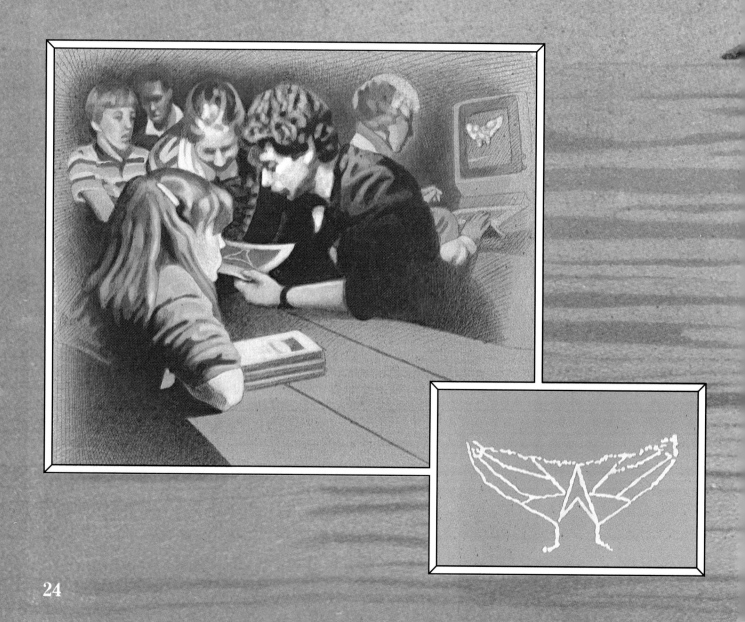

Anne explained. "It's a program we're working on to help us identify whales." She pointed to the drawing of the flukes on the computer screen. "The flukes are divided into fourteen sectors. For each sector, I look at the photograph and tell the computer if the sector is mostly black or white and if it has any markings."

Arthur was catching on. "And the computer stores the same information that's in the fluke catalogue?"

"Right! The computer quickly compares all the information for all the sectors and gives us a list of the most likely matches. We still have to make the final choices by eye."

"Here's the computer's list," Anne said as she punched a key and up came a list of numbers. At the top was 0159.

"Hey, look! I told you!" C.T. cried.

Sally Ruth knew it all along. "He's right. That's 'Fringe,' 0159."

Ramon nodded. "We've seen her three years in a row."

"Yahoo!" shouted C.T. "No dishes for a week!"

This was too much for Rachel. "Get out of here, you lucky little creep!" But she couldn't help smiling.

It had been a long and exciting day. *Mimi* rode quietly on the calm sea. Everyone except Captain Granville had turned in. But it was hard to sleep.

Arthur's head spun with everything he'd learned on his first day at sea. "Man, I can't wait 'til tomorrow."

C.T. was not even homesick. "I wonder if we'll see more whales."

The boat creaked and rocked gently. Ramon smiled. "You never know. G'night, you guys. Good job today."

It's a Fluke!

There is a real humpback whale 0159 named Fringe.

Estimated length: 12.8 meters
Estimated weight: 36.4 metric tons

Whale researchers have observed Fringe in the Gulf of Maine for several years. In 1979 and 1980 she was with her calf, Tassel; in 1981 she was alone; in 1982 she was with a new calf, Sirius, thought to be a male.*

Do you recognize the top photo? It is the fluke shot of Fringe that C.T. matched in the fluke catalogue. Look at the other four photos. Which one is another view of Fringe's flukes? Match the flukes in the top photo with the flukes in one of the photos below.

How did you make your match?

1. Which part of the photo did you look at first?
2. Which information was most helpful—the fluke shapes, the colorings, the markings?
3. What convinced you of your choice?

No two whales have the same fluke patterns. And no two human beings have the same thumbprints. Two of the prints on this page belong to the same person. Which two prints match?

*Data courtesy of Cetacean Research program, Provincetown Center for Coastal Studies, Provincetown, MA.

26

How Big is a Whale?

A. How well would a whale fit into your world? To find out, compare Fringe with a school bus and a car. (Hint: Measure the length of each drawing. Then multiply the length by the number of meters per centimeter shown in the scale.) Exactly how big are the other figures compared with a humpback whale?

B. How do *you* measure up to Fringe? On a separate piece of paper, make a scale drawing of yourself. Cut it out and place it on the page near the other figures. How big are *you* compared to a humpback? How many times bigger than you is Fringe?

Scale: 1 centimeter = 1 meter

C. An average-sized humpback weighs about 36 metric tons. How many kilograms do you weigh? How many children of your weight would equal the weight of one humpback whale? (Hint: Change metric tons to kilograms. Then divide the whale's weight by your weight.)

D. Find out the weights of other animals: elephant, dinosaur, horse, cow, and dog. Figure out how many of each animal equal the weight of one humpback whale.

WHALEWATCH

Mark Graham is an actor. He plays the part of Arthur Spencer in "The Voyage of the *Mimi*." Like Arthur, Mark is a high school senior. But Mark lives in South Natick, Massachusetts, not in the Bronx, New York, as Arthur does. Mark enjoyed playing Arthur because he got to travel and meet interesting people. Best of all, he got to see lots of whales.

Carole Carlson and Stormy (his real name is Charles) Mayo are marine biologists who study whales. Mark visited the two scientists in Provincetown, Massachusetts. Stormy is a founder of the Provincetown Center for Coastal Studies, where he and Carole work. Both are real-life models for the characters of Anne and Ramon, and they worked with the writers of "The Voyage of the *Mimi*" to help make the show realistic.

Carole met Mark at the bus station. As they walked back to the Center for Coastal Studies, Carole told Mark why she thought it was important to study whales. "By studying them and learning more about them, I think we can help to protect them from extinction."

"What would happen if all of them did die?" Mark asked. "I like whales, but some people just say 'so what?' How do you answer them?"

Carole responded, "We don't know how the disappearance of a *species* will affect the environment until it happens. Whales are at the top of their *food chain*, which means that they eat many animals, but few animals eat them. So if all the whales did disappear, we might see a big increase in the populations of the animals they eat. And though we wouldn't see another group of animals die off because their food—the whales—had disappeared, the loss would be very great. An important order of animals would have gone without our

knowing what we could have learned from them.

"The whales are, in a sense, representative of all *endangered* species," continued Carole. "Some people may find it hard to care about a fish or an insect that is becoming extinct, but I think most people have felt the plight of the whales. Whales and other creatures deserve to live here, just as we do."

"Of course," said Mark, "I agree with that."

"Human beings are polluting the ocean. By spreading the word about the whales, we hope to create concern for the ocean It's the whales' environment," Carole said.

Stormy was waiting for Carole and Mark when they arrived at the Center. He was hoping that Mark could help him sort out some of the data that had been gathered during the summer months. Mark was happy to help. It was the same kind of work Arthur does on the *Mimi*. Mark knew a lot about humpbacks, but not much about the other kinds of whales. He took advantage of Stormy's knowledge to learn more about them.

Stormy first explained that there are two basic groups of whales. There are whales with teeth, called *odontocetes*, and whales with baleen, called *mysticetes*. How whales get and eat their food depends on whether they have teeth or baleen. Toothed whales use their teeth to grab a fish or a squid, and then they swallow it whole. Baleen whales also swallow their food whole, but their food is small and they scoop up a lot of it at once. Baleen is made of the same material as our fingernails. To get food, a baleen whale closes its mouth

The blue whale at the top and the gray whale on the left are baleen whales. Baleen hangs from the whale's upper jaw in closely packed plates. The plates are shredded on the inner side and look like coarse hair.

on lots of small fish or shrimp, and water. Then it uses its huge tongue to press all the water out through the baleen. The hairy inside surface of the baleen traps the fish or shrimp, and the whale then swallows its large meal.

The smallest baleen whale is the minke whale, which measures 30 feet long at most. But this group includes the largest creature ever to live on earth—the blue whale. As with all baleen whales, female blue whales are larger than the males. Full-grown blue whales range in length from 50 to 100 feet. One is on record as having weighed 197 tons, although most weigh less than that. Blue whales have almost been wiped out by hunters. They seem to be shy animals, and since there are so few left, blue whales are rarely seen.

Gray whales, too, were almost wiped out by hunters. In 1947, they became protected by law as an endangered species. Since then, they have made a remarkable comeback. Now large numbers of gray whales can be seen swimming up and down the Pacific coast between Alaska and Baja California on their annual migration, which is the longest of any mammal known. Unlike other baleen whales, gray whales feed along shallow ocean bottoms, scooping up creatures that live in the sand. Full-grown gray whales are 40 to 50 feet, and may weigh 30 to 40 tons.

Another kind of baleen whale is the right whale. Whale hunters gave this animal its name because it was the "right" whale to hunt: it was slow moving and easy to catch, floated when killed, and yielded large amounts of oil. Right whales look different from most other whales because of their enormous heads, very curved mouths, and rounder bodies. They grow to about 50 feet in length, but may weigh as much as 60 or 70 tons. Of all of the baleen whales, right whales are the most endangered. There may be fewer than 4,000 in the world. Individual right whales are identified by the pattern of white, wartlike *callosities* which appear as spots on the whales' heads.

29

All the whales shown on these two pages are toothed whales. Toothed whales travel in herds, or pods, and have very sophisticated social orders. If a member of their group is in danger or is injured, the others will stay with it to protect it or help it breathe.

The sperm whale is the largest of the other group of whales, the toothed whales. Moby Dick was a sperm whale. Generally, male toothed whales are larger than the females. Female sperm whales may grow 35 to 40 feet in length, while the males may reach 60 feet. They travel in family groups composed of one large male with many females and their young. Sperm whales spend most of their time in warm waters near the equator. They eat giant squid and dive to great depths to find them. Sperm whales dive deeper than any other whale. Special adjustable chambers and fluids inside their large heads make this possible. Each individual sperm whale makes a unique series of clicking sounds. Sperm whales have the largest brains (15 to 20 pounds) of any creature on earth.

Many people have heard of killer whales and are afraid of them. These beautiful toothed whales, better known as orcas, eat seals and small whales, but have never been known to harm humans. They have huge fins on their backs and travel in large family groups known as *pods*. Female orcas may be as small as 15 feet in length, and male orcas as large as 30 feet.

Some people are surprised to learn that dol-phins and porpoises are whales. The most common of toothed whales, there are over 60 species of dolphins and porpoises. They inhabit nearly every ocean of the world, and some rivers and lakes as well. Dolphins almost always travel in pods, and have a very sophisticated social order. They aid an injured one of their kind by supporting the hurt dolphin and helping it to breathe. They seem to be playful animals, and many lonely sailors have been comforted by the sight of dolphins playing alongside their boat. Like all whales, dolphins are extremely smart animals.

Narwhals and belugas are two kinds of toothed whales that live only in Arctic waters. Both are unusual. The most distinctive feature of the narwhal is its single long tusk, extending six to nine feet out from the animal's upper lip. The tusk, which is really a tooth, is found only on the males. Many people think that the narwhal may be the inspiration for the legend of the unicorn. Narwhals attain a length of 13 to 15 feet.

Belugas, slightly smaller than narwhals, are completely white. Seen in the Arctic among icebergs, they resemble bobbing chunks of ice. They are quite vocal, and chatter to each other. Belugas

have a very round forehead. They can actually change the shape of their forehead and adjust it to make the different sounds they use for *echolocation*.

Echolocation is a talent shared by all toothed whales. These animals make sounds that hit and then bounce off objects around them. When they hear the echoes of these sounds, the whales know where they are and what is around them. In this way they navigate and find food. Toothed whales do have eyes, but seeing is not always easy because light does not penetrate very deeply in water. However, sound travels well through water; better than through the air, in fact. With their built-in echo sounders, toothed whales can find their way, even in the dark.

Carole and Stormy don't stay on land long if the weather is nice. So, even though it was November, they decided to head out to Stellwagen Bank in their research vessel and look for whales. Mark would have liked to go with them, but he had to get back home. Mark was sorry to leave Provincetown and felt a little sad to say goodbye to Stormy and Carole. Most of all, he was sorry to leave the whales. He knew it would be many months before he saw them again.

Hippopotamuses are huge, plant-eating mammals. Like whales, hippos are at the top of their food chain. Recently, the disappearance of a hippopotamus herd from an African river had a disastrous effect. A river bank breaks down under the weight of hippos moving over it. In this case, their trails allowed rain water to drain off the land. When the hippos were killed off because of their danger to people, the river bank ceased to be broken down. Water stayed on the land, and the wet land promoted the growth of a slug that carries a disease deadly to humans.

Draw a scientific conclusion from this story.

ON THE SHOALS

On the second day out of Gloucester, the *Mimi* continued on a course toward Georges Bank, the humpback whales' main feeding ground in the Gulf of Maine. Sally Ruth was giving Arthur a lesson in steering the boat. Rachel was in the *crosstrees* looking for whales.

"Are you sure you don't see any whales?" C.T. called to Rachel from the deck.

"Don't worry, C.T.," she replied. "If I spot any whales, you'll be the first to know!"

Ramon came up on deck to call the crew to breakfast. "Uh-oh," he said, seeing Arthur at the wheel. "Do you have your driver's license?"

"Nothing to it," Arthur said. "It's like a big video game."

Sally Ruth tapped him on the shoulder and pointed to the *binnacle*. While he was joking around with Ramon, he had let the *Mimi* stray off course.

"Keep it on one-two-zero," Sally Ruth instructed him.

Below, the Captain explained their course to Anne. C.T. joined them.

"We're here," said Captain Gran-ville, indicating a point on the naviga-chart. "We're on a course heading one-two-zero. We'll continue on this until we get to the northwest of Georges Bank. Just before shoals . . ."

"I know what shoals are," C.T. interrupted. "Shallow water."

"Just before these, uh, shallow waters," the Captain continued, "we'll make a course change to come through this *channel*."

"Good," Anne agreed. "The hump-backs could be feeding anywhere along the bank. How long until we reach the shoals?"

The Captain used *dividers* to measure the distance on the chart. "That's exactly fifty miles," he said. Then he looked up at the *knotmeter* to check the speed. "That's funny," he said. "I thought we were going a little faster than that. Anyway, at a steady speed of five *knots*, it will be another ten hours before we reach the shoals."

"What's a knot?" C.T. asked.

Anne explained. "A knot is a measurement of speed, C.T. One knot is one nautical mile per hour."

Captain Granville tapped the knotmeter.

"Is there a problem?" Anne asked.

"Those shoals are really very tricky waters," the Captain answered. "I'd just as soon get through that channel before dark."

The Captain went up on deck, and C.T. took a closer look at the chart. "Holy cow!" he exclaimed, pointing to a spot on Georges Bank. "It says there are unexploded depth charges here. What if we hit one?" he asked Ramon.

"It's not likely," Ramon answered, taking a look at the chart. "See these numbers? They indicate depths. Those explosives are one hundred twenty-six *fathoms* down. A fathom is six feet, so that's . . ."

"Seven hundred and fifty-six feet of moving water," moaned Arthur, who was feeling seasick.

"Arthur," Anne said, "you don't look so good. You'd better get up on deck."

Rachel had her own idea about how to cure seasickness. "Here, Arthur," she said, placing a sandwich in front of him. "Take a big bite of this—peanut butter, banana, raisins, and chocolate sauce."

Anne could hardly believe what she was seeing. "Rachel!" she admonished.

But it was too late. The sight of the gooey concoction sent Arthur rushing up on deck.

"Rachel," Anne said firmly, "that was a rotten thing to do."

"I know," said Rachel, confidently taking a bite out of the sandwich, "but he'll feel a lot better now."

On deck, Arthur was hanging over the rail when C.T. emerged from below. He glanced uneasily at Arthur.

"Am I going to get sick, too?" he asked his grandfather, who was at the wheel.

"Probably."

"What about you?" C.T. continued.

"I only get sick on land," the Captain answered gruffly.

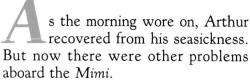As the morning wore on, Arthur recovered from his seasickness. But now there were other problems aboard the *Mimi*.

Anne was having trouble with the computer. It kept crashing—blinking out—in the middle of her work. This report made Captain Granville wonder about the other instruments. He glanced at the knotmeter. It still indicated a speed of five knots.

Grabbing a slice of bread and his stopwatch, the Captain went up on deck. He enlisted Rachel's help in using an old seafarer's method to check the *Mimi*'s speed.

He tossed the slice of bread into the water off the bow of the boat. Using the stopwatch, Rachel measured the time it took the *stern* of the boat to pass the floating bread. With that information, the Captain was able to estimate the *Mimi*'s actual speed.

"How fast are we going?"

"About six and a half knots," the Captain replied to Rachel.

"Something's not right." He called below to Anne. "Miss Abrams, what does the *echo sounder* read?"

Anne looked at the instrument. "Around twenty-one fathoms deep. But I don't trust that reading."

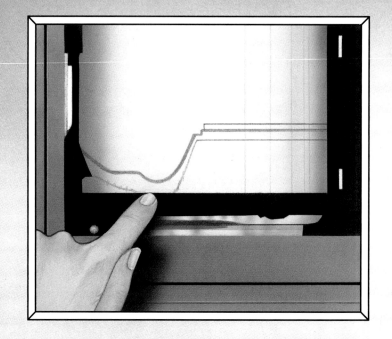

"What is that thing, anyhow?" C.T. asked her.

"An echo sounder measures how deep the water is under the boat," Anne explained. "It sends down sound waves to the bottom and measures the time they take to bounce back up. But I think something's wrong with the echo sounder." Pointing to the echo sounder *profile*, she noted, "This line is too flat. It should look more uneven, like this line indicating depth readings made earlier."

On deck, the Captain took over the wheel from Sally Ruth. "Rachel," he ordered, "tell Ramon to bring up the *lead line*."

Rachel returned a few seconds later carrying a long rope with a weight tied to one end.

"I told you to get Ramon!" the Captain said impatiently.

"I can do this," Rachel insisted. "I've done it lots of times."

There was no time to waste arguing, and the Captain consented. "Hurry it up," he said.

From the *starboard* bow, Rachel tossed the weighted end of the line overboard. When it hit bottom, the length of the rope that had gone into the water indicated the depth.

"Uh-oh! Two fathoms!" she called to Captain Granville.

The *Mimi* was in dangerously shallow water. The Captain had to act quickly.

"Take the wheel, Sally Ruth! Turn her into the wind!"

Rushing below, he instructed Ramon to get the sails down fast, and get the anchor ready.

"What's wrong?" Anne asked.

"We've got an electrical problem. The instruments are all misreading. We've been going faster than the knotmeter indicates, and we're farther along our course than I wanted."

"We're on the shoals?" C.T. asked anxiously.

"Yep," his grandfather said, switching on the *radio direction finder* tuner and adjusting the dial. "I'll find our location with the RDF. It has batteries."

On deck, the Captain instructed Arthur in the use of the RDF. "Turn the unit until the signal you hear gets weakest. That means the antenna is pointing directly at the radio beacon I tuned in when I was below. The compass reading you see on top gives you the *bearing* to the beacon. This one is two hundred eighty-five degrees. I'm going below to tune in a second beacon. Turn the antenna until the signal is weakest, then call out the compass reading to me."

A few minutes later, Captain Granville pinpointed the ship's location based on the RDF readings. "The bearing to the first beacon was two hundred eighty-five degrees," he said, using the parallel rulers to draw a line on the chart. "And here's the one Arthur just gave me—three hundred thirty-four degrees." He drew the second line. "Where these lines *intersect*, or cross, is where we are," he concluded, pointing to the chart. "Right here on Georges Shoals. And that's bad."

The crew had just finished getting the sails down when the Captain broke the bad news. "We'll anchor here for the night," he said. "We'll have to head for port in the morning."

Rachel and Sally Ruth couldn't hide their disappointment.

"It can't be helped," Anne said. "We can't sail without instruments," Ramon added.

Meanwhile, Arthur was checking the *Mimi*'s electrical system. In the engine room, he opened a *fuse box* and found sparks shooting out from one of the connections. Quickly, he threw the main switch, and shut off the electricity all over the boat.

"What's going on?" the Captain demanded, storming across the deck.

"Captain Granville, I did that," said Arthur as he stuck his head out of the engine room *hatch*.

"Who said you could go down there?" the Captain shouted angrily.

"I think I found the problem," explained Arthur, avoiding the Captain's question.

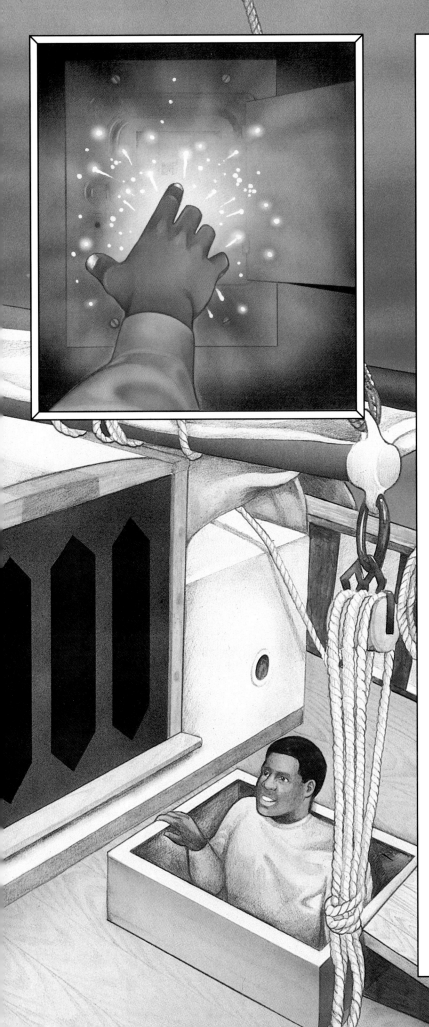

"You don't touch any of the equipment on this boat without checking with me first!"

Anne intervened. "Captain Granville, Arthur does know about electricity. His father's an electrician."

The Captain paused. "Okay, show me!"

In the engine room, Arthur showed the Captain the source of the problem. "Someone put in a piece of copper tubing instead of a fuse," he said. "There's a short circuit somewhere. Without the fuse, these connections got so hot they're melting." He removed the tubing.

"That could cause a real fire down here," the Captain said.

"If you've got the right tools," Arthur suggested, "I think we can fix it."

"Grandpa," the boy asked, "if you can't fix it, can I go back to Ohio?"

Aggravated by the electrical problem, the Captain had no patience left. "C.T.," he said sharply, "we've got this whole summer to get through together, no matter what happens. So stay out of the way!"

While Arthur used a *multimeter* to check the *Mimi*'s electrical equipment for the short circuit, Captain Granville worked to repair the damage to the junction box. In the *saloon,* the rest of the crew waited in the dark to see if the voyage would continue.

The Captain had just inserted a new fuse into the fuse box when Arthur returned to the engine room.

"The electric *winch* shorted out," he reported, "so I disconnected it."

"Good," the Captain said. Then, after testing the fuse with the multimeter, he continued, "It looks good, Arthur. Shall I give it a try?"

Arthur nodded and the Captain threw the main power switch. Instantly, lights went on all over the *Mimi*.

Arthur and the Captain were greeted with cheers when they entered the saloon.

"So we're on the road again?" Rachel asked.

"Yep," the Captain declared, slapping Arthur on the back. "The kid knows what he's doing."

While the others celebrated, C.T. slipped away quietly and went up on deck. Sally Ruth followed. She found him curled up dejectedly in the dory.

"Are you homesick, C.T.?" she asked sympathetically.

C.T. could hold back his feelings no longer. "I don't like it here," he blurted out tearfully. "Sailing's dumb! They said Grandpa wanted to see me. They said I could help him. But it's not true. I don't know anything about sailing, and he doesn't want to see me!"

"C.T., your grandfather really loves you," Sally Ruth insisted. "He just has trouble showing it."

"He sure does," C.T. agreed.

"Here, I'll teach you something," Sally Ruth said. Using American Sign Language she signed: We're friends. "You try it," she urged.

Hesitantly, C.T. imitated the sign. Then, he smiled. "Friends," he confirmed.

"And tomorrow," Sally Ruth reminded him, speaking and signing, "whales!"

Sally Ruth went below and C.T. remained alone in the dory. Suddenly, his thoughts were interrupted by the great loud whooshing sound of a whale surfacing right next to the *Mimi*.

Excited, C.T. climbed out of the dory. Running to tell the others and rejoin the warm circle of friends, he shouted, "Hey, everybody . . .!"

Time At Sea

If C.T. kept a journal of Episode 3 of "The Voyage of the *Mimi*," it might read something like this:

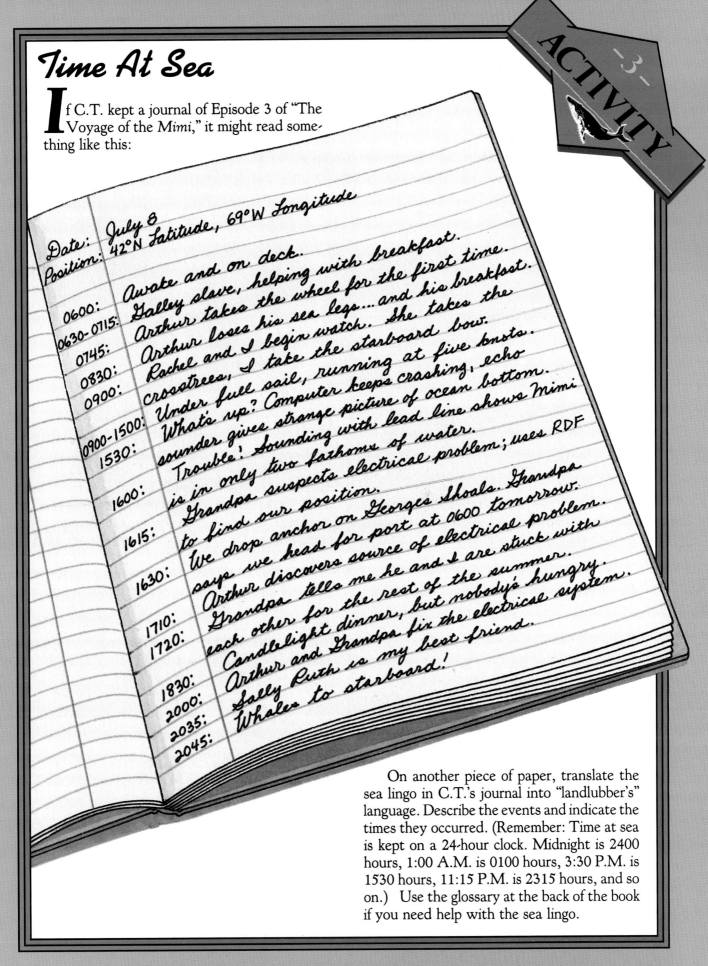

Date: July 8
Position: 42°N Latitude, 69°W Longitude

0600: Awake and on deck.

0630-0715: Galley slave, helping with breakfast.

0745: Arthur takes the wheel for the first time.

0830: Arthur loses his sea legs...and his breakfast.

0900: Rachel and I begin watch. She takes the crosstrees, I take the starboard bow.

0900-1500: Under full sail, running at five knots.

1530: What's up? Computer keeps crashing, echo sounder gives strange picture of ocean bottom.

1600: Trouble! Sounding with lead line shows Mimi is in only two fathoms of water.

1615: Grandpa suspects electrical problem; uses RDF to find our position.

1630: We drop anchor on Georges Shoals. Grandpa says we head for port at 0600 tomorrow.

1710: Arthur discovers source of electrical problem.

1720: Grandpa tells me he and I are stuck with each other for the rest of the summer.

1830: Candlelight dinner, but nobody's hungry.

2000: Arthur and Grandpa fix the electrical system.

2035: Sally Ruth is my best friend.

2045: Whales to starboard!

On another piece of paper, translate the sea lingo in C.T.'s journal into "landlubber's" language. Describe the events and indicate the times they occurred. (Remember: Time at sea is kept on a 24-hour clock. Midnight is 2400 hours, 1:00 A.M. is 0100 hours, 3:30 P.M. is 1530 hours, 11:15 P.M. is 2315 hours, and so on.) Use the glossary at the back of the book if you need help with the sea lingo.

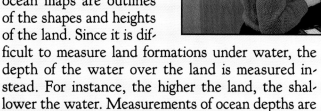

Dr. Kim Kastens explained a bathymetric map to Mary.

The crew members on board the *Mimi* use nautical charts to help them navigate. Nautical charts are ocean maps. Like land maps, ocean maps are outlines of the shapes and heights of the land. Since it is difficult to measure land formations under water, the depth of the water over the land is measured instead. For instance, the higher the land, the shallower the water. Measurements of ocean depths are called *soundings*.

For centuries, ocean maps were based on soundings taken with a lead line. The maps were not very accurate. Nowadays, scientists have more accurate ways of taking ocean soundings. As a result, they have more accurate ocean maps.

Mary Tanner is the actress who plays Rachel Fairbanks in "The Voyage of the *Mimi*." During the summer that she worked on the show, Mary met Kim Kastens. Kim is a marine geologist who studies and maps the bottom of the ocean. The maps show what the bottom would look like if all the water were drained out.

Mary visited Kim at the Lamont-Doherty Geological Observatory in Palisades, New York, in order to learn more about Kim's work. There Mary saw an oceanographer's map – a world map of the ocean bottom. She was surprised to learn that the earth under water looks very much like the earth above the water. On the ocean floor there are hills, valleys, canyons, plains and even mountain chains. Some mountain chains are as high as the Andes or the Rockies. The deepest place in the ocean, and in the world, is the Marianas Trench, which is 11,000 meters deep, or nearly seven miles.

Making a map of the sea floor requires days or even months of ship time. The ship is driven back and forth over a small area to take measurements of the distance from the ocean surface to the ocean floor. The measurements are made with an *echo sounder*. This instrument sends sound pulses down to the sea floor. The sea floor reflects the sound back to the ship. The echo sounder records the time it takes for the sound pulses to reach the sea floor and echo back to the ship on the surface. Then it computes the water depth in that spot based on the speed of sound through water.

As the ship moves over the sea floor, the repeated measurements of water depths are plotted as a *profile*. At sea, it is Kim's job to help gather depth measurements. Back at Lamont-Doherty, it is her job to turn these measurements into a map. Mary helped Kim make a map of the sea floor.

Work on the map began by Kim showing Mary how to use a computer to draw a chart of the ship's path. The computer chart shows where the ship was every 15 minutes as it moved along its path. The echo-sounder profile shows water depths along the ship's path. Both the computer chart and the profile show date and time information. By matching date and time information on both charts, Kim and Mary could write the correct water depth on the chart where that depth was measured. When all the numbers were written in, Mary drew lines connecting places that had the same depth. On a map, these lines are called *contour lines*.

To make the contour map easier to read, the women colored the map. Kim said it was traditional to make the most shallow areas the brightest colors. So they started with yellow at a shallow plateau that was 2,600 meters deep. They finished with dark blues and purples in the deepest areas, more than 4,000 meters below the water surface.

Coloring the map took Kim and Mary all morning. When they were finished they had a beautiful contour map of an area of the ocean floor. On the world map, Kim showed Mary how much of the ocean bottom their map represented – an area the size of a postage stamp. It also represented five days of ship work. Mary began to appreciate the amount of work that had gone into making the world map. How was it done?

Kim explained that in some areas of the ocean, there have been many oceanographic voyages and the depth data is good. These areas are usually near major shipping lanes, or near large population centers. But for other parts of the ocean, scientists have little information. This is because these areas are remote, and it is difficult to make an expedition there. For these areas, mapmakers must guess at what lies in between the echo sounder tracks they do have.

The echo sounder profile is a cross section, or side view, of the sea floor along the ship's path.

On their contour map, Kim and Mary made areas of equal depth the same color. Kim said it was traditional to make the shallowest areas the brightest colors.

Bill Haxby used satellite data to compile a computer map of the world's sea floor. He can use the computer to zoom in on certain areas of the map and examine mountains and trenches that no one knew even existed.

There is a need for faster methods of mapping bigger areas of the sea floor. Kim introduced Mary to Bill Haxby, a geophysicist, who has devised such a method. Bill spends a lot of time at a computer terminal. He works on maps of the world's sea floor using satellite data rather than shipboard data.

This is how his method works. A satellite called Seasat was launched in 1978 with a device on it called an *altimeter*. The altimeter is a little bit like an echo sounder. But instead of using sound pulses, the altimeter uses microwaves. The altimeter measures the time it takes for the microwaves to make a round trip from 800 kilometers (about 500 miles) in space to the sea surface instead of to the sea floor.

The sea surface is not as flat as it appears to the eye. In reality the surface has bumps and dips, with height differences as great as 170 meters. Bill figured out that the bumps and dips show differences in gravity. For example, a mountain has greater gravitational force than a valley. So, the water bunches up over a mountain and forms a depression over a place like the Marianas Trench.

A satellite can measure the ocean depth much more rapidly than a ship can. From just three months' worth of Seasat data, Bill has a sea floor map of most of the world. Using his mapping technique, he discovered some huge undersea mountains that no one ever knew about.

Mary wondered why scientists go through the slow process of making a map from echo soundings instead of using satellites. Kim explained that Bill's method of mapping is very broad, very general. His maps may indicate large land forms that need to be studied by marine geologists. But the best way to study these previously unknown land forms is to collect information during shipboard cruises and then make detailed contour maps.

When Mary left Lamont-Doherty Geological Observatory, she knew that she would never again look at the ocean in the same way.

Pressure is a property of water. The deeper the water, the greater the pressure. To find the approximate water pressure at a given depth, use this formula: depth in feet ÷ 2 = pressure in pounds per square inch.

As divers descend to a depth of a little less than 1 meter in water, they feel a popping sensation in their ears. To go slightly deeper for any length of time, they need air tanks to breathe. At a depth greater than 133 meters, humans are crushed unless they are in an underwater ship. One kind of underwater ship is called a bathyscaphe. Inside a bathyscaphe named the *Trieste*, some scientists went down to the Marianas Trench, the deepest place in the ocean, in 1960. The depth of the Marianas Trench is about 11,000 meters. The *Trieste* dove to 10,910 meters.

Can you suggest a reason why mapping expeditions to the deep are so difficult?

On the third day of the voyage, the sun rose over a calm sea. Captain Granville came up on deck and found C.T. tying knots in a length of rope.

"Where did you learn all those knots?" the Captain asked.

"Pa taught me. He knows how to tie a lot of knots."

"I know," the Captain said. "I taught him." He paused for a moment, then added, "Come with me, boy."

In the captain's quarters, Captain Granville removed a small battered notebook from his desk.

"This is a whaler's journal," he explained. "It's sort of a diary. It belonged to my grandfather – your great-great grandfather. He went to sea when he was just about your age and wrote the journal when he wasn't much older."

C.T. opened the book and was surprised to see hand-drawn pictures of whales at the bottom of a page.

"That's how they recorded the whales they struck. Whaling was a big industry in this area then. Many whales were killed. Some *species*, like the humpback, were killed off almost to *extinction*. Keep the journal below deck, C.T. Someday it will be yours."

In the galley and saloon, the rest of the crew was assembling for breakfast.

"Captain Granville," Anne said, showing him the nautical chart, "this is the area of Georges Bank where we want to start our *census*."

"Today, we'll make four *transects*," Sally Ruth explained, "each on a straight-line course." And she pointed to four straight lines on the chart.

"As the boat travels along each course," Anne continued, "we'll count and collect data on the whales we see. We want to travel at a constant speed of five knots. Humpbacks swim at three or four knots. We don't want any to pass us, or we might count them twice."

The Captain nodded. "Let's weigh anchor," he said. "All hands on deck!"

"We're at 67 degrees, 42 minutes west longitude, 41 degrees, 30 minutes north *latitude*," C.T. said.

Anne checked her watch. "Okay, start counting!"

"One, two, three," Arthur joked.

The crew scanned the ocean, as the *Mimi* continued on the first transect with no humpbacks in sight.

"Hey, ONE!" Arthur called. "I mean there really is one!" He pointed to a cloud of spray in the distance.

"Sighting cue?" Anne asked. "That means, what did you see first?"

"Blow," Arthur answered.

"Bearing?"

"Fifty-six degrees."

"Distance?"

"Uh . . . four hundred meters," Arthur said uncertainly.

Anne pulled on a rope that ran up to the crosstrees where Sally Ruth was. The rope movement got her attention.

"How far?" Anne signed.

"Eight hundred meters," Sally Ruth replied looking out toward the whale.

"Way to go, Spencer," Rachel jibed.

"You'll get the hang of it," Ramon reassured Arthur. "Just remember that on a clear day, the horizon is about five miles, or eight kilometers."

"I got one over here!" Rachel called out from her position in the rigging. "I spotted the blow at 115 degrees, and it's about 650 meters out."

"I'd say that's just about right, Rachel," Ramon said. "But there's only one problem."

"That's not a humpback," Sally Ruth called from the crosstrees.

"It's a finback!" Ramon said.

As the whale broke the surface, Ramon pointed out its distinguishing *characteristics*. "It's bigger than a humpback, the dorsal fin is sharper, and when it dives, it doesn't hump its back like . . ."

"Like a humpback," Rachel said wryly.

As the morning passed, the *Mimi* continued its first transect of Georges Bank. More whales were sighted, and Anne recorded the data: *time, bearing, distance, behavior,* and *species.* When the transect was completed, she entered the data into the computer. A diagram appeared on the screen, showing the boat's course and the locations of whales sighted within two miles on either side of the course.

"Only eight whales," Arthur said. "That doesn't seem like very many."

"Look at it this way," Ramon pointed out. "This transect represents a ten-mile strip of ocean, four miles wide. That's 40 square miles. The bank is about 12,000 square miles. Eight humpbacks for every 40 square miles, that would be . . . "

". . . 2,400 humpbacks," Arthur calculated. "That's impossible, right?"

"It's not likely," said Anne. "The humpback population in the northwest Atlantic isn't more than 2,400."

"Maybe the humpbacks are doing better than we thought," Rachel said.

"It's more likely that whales concentrate in certain areas of the bank," Ramon explained. "That's why we'll be doing a series of transects in different parts of the bank."

The whale census continued throughout the day. Data was collected for every whale sighted during three more transects of that area of Georges Bank. It was exciting to see the whales. But there were long periods of waiting when no whales were in sight. The work was hard and sometimes tedious.

After the fourth transect, Anne announced, "That's it for today."

The crew members welcomed the chance to stretch their muscles. Suddenly, "More whales ahead!" Sally Ruth called out, and pointed to a group of humpbacks in the distance. The sight of the whales made the crew members forget their weariness.

Ramon said, "We can't count them in this census. But we sure can look!"

Motioning toward the crosstrees, C.T. asked Captain Granville, "Can I go up now, Grandpa? I climb trees taller than that all the time at home."

"Trees stand still," the Captain replied gruffly.

"But Sally Ruth asked me," C.T. insisted. "She said I could help her spot whales to photograph."

Captain Granville looked at the boy's earnest face. "See that safety line over there? Tie it around your chest. Make sure it's good and tight."

Ramon took the wheel. Captain Granville held the safety line as C.T. slowly climbed the *rigging* up to the crosstrees, 50 feet above the deck.

While C.T. climbed up, the others gathered at the rail as the whales approached. The humpbacks seemed unafraid and almost friendly.

"I can't believe they're so close," Rachel said, "and so trusting."

One whale lingered at the surface just inches from the *Mimi*'s hull. Ramon pointed to the broad, bumpy area on top of the whale's massive head.

"That's called the *rostrum*," he said.

"What are those bumps?" Arthur asked.

"They're *tubercles*," Ramon explained. "There's a little stiff hair on each bump. The ancestors of whales lived on land and were covered with hair, like most *mammals*. The hair on the tubercles is all that's left."

"Are those *barnacles* on its chin?" Rachel asked.

"Yes. Barnacles grow on the chin patch, flippers, and flukes."

"Do they hurt the whale?"

"We don't know," said Ramon.

Another whale surfaced nearby and blew a *spume* of mist into the air.

"See how the whale closes its blowhole just before the water gets in?" Anne pointed out.

"It has its nose on top of its head!" said Arthur.

"That's a good place to have one if you live underwater," Anne said.

From their vantage point in the crosstrees, Sally Ruth and C.T. could see how big the whales are. The long white flippers of the humpbacks looked like airplane wings as the whales glided gracefully around and under the *Mimi*.

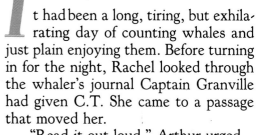

It had been a long, tiring, but exhilarating day of counting whales and just plain enjoying them. Before turning in for the night, Rachel looked through the whaler's journal Captain Granville had given C.T. She came to a passage that moved her.

"Read it out loud," Arthur urged.

"It's kind of sad," Rachel cautioned.

"Go on," C.T. said.

"Well, okay," she agreed. " 'The whale was close by the ship. It lay there, playing about, as if all unconscious of the near danger. It was so near us that I had a fine chance of seeing all that was done. I saw them when they threw the two irons into it. Then he thrashed about in the water and took the boat along with him at a rate I should not fancy going. I could see him as he went along, throwing first his flukes and then his head out of the water, and then spouting a stream of blood into the air. I could see the whale was getting weaker, and its motions were less frequent and fainter. It was soon dead and the two boats were not long towing it to the ship.' "

In the silence that followed, the haunting images from the journal mingled with the group's recent memories of the gentle, trusting humpbacks.

Finally, Rachel said good night quietly, and left for her quarters.

"Come on, buddy," Arthur said seeing the sadness in C.T.'s face. "Let's get some sleep." And he turned out the light.

In the darkness, C.T. murmured, "The whalers must have been right next to the whales, just like we were."

Making Sense of a Census

One of the goals of the *Mimi* scientists was a whale census—counting the whale population—of Georges Bank. The census was taken by making a series of transects, or crossings, in at least six different parts of the Bank and counting the whales sighted.

The table below contains census information about six series of transects on Georges Bank. Use the information to estimate the total number of humpbacks in the Georges Bank population.

Transect series no.	No. of transects	×	No. of mi per transect	×	Sighting range per transect*	=	No. of sq mi covered	No. of humpbacks sighted
1	4		10		4		160	21
2	3		12		4			15
3	1		25		4			9
4	2		6		4			10
5	4		8		4			13
6	3		10		4			16

*Sighting range is 2 miles on either side of the boat, a total of 4 miles.

To estimate the total humpback population on Georges Bank, follow these steps:

1. Calculate the number of square miles covered in each transect series. (The first one has been done for you: 4 transects × 10 miles per transect × 4 miles sighting range = 4 × 10 × 4 = 160 square miles.)

2. Calculate the total number of square miles covered in all six transect series.

3. Calculate the total number of humpbacks sighted in all six transect series.

4. Calculate the average number of humpbacks sighted for every square mile of Georges Bank covered. (Hint: Divide the total number of humpbacks sighted by the total number of square miles covered.)

5. Calculate the estimated humpback population on Georges Bank. (Hint: Multiply the average number of humpbacks per square mile times the total number of square miles on Georges Bank. Georges Bank covers an area of about 12,000 square miles.)

Why do you think it's important to do a series of transects in many areas of the Bank instead of just one? What if you had to base your census estimate only on transect series 3? on transect series 4?

WHALE BONES

To the *Mimi* crew, who has a chance to look at whales up close, whales certainly don't look like fish. But still it seems a little odd that they are mammals. After all, they do live in the ocean. And, as Ramon explains, their ancestors once walked on land. Ben Affleck, who plays C.T., found these facts very puzzling. In order to learn more about the natural history of whales, Ben visited a couple of scientists at the Smithsonian Institution in Washington, D.C.

At the Smithsonian Museum of Natural History, Ben saw a fiber glass model of a blue whale—the largest animal ever to live on earth.

time. The rest of the collection is carefully stored for use by scholars and scientists from around the world who go to the Museum of Natural History to do research. Because any one example of a plant or animal is special in some way, scientists need to study many samples of the same species.

The Smithsonian Institution is the museum for the nation. The Institution's many museums contain over 100 million specimens and artifacts. One museum, the Museum of Natural History, has 81 million of them. For instance, this museum has over 7 million beetles, 4 million butterflies and moths, 114,429 birds' eggs, 110,764 rocks, 35,594 human skeletons, 8,000 turtles, 6,106 shrimp, 4,500 meteorites, and 14 elephant skeletons. It's a big museum. Only one percent of those 81 million specimens and artifacts is on public display at any

The first person Ben met at the Museum of Natural History was Charlie Potter. Charlie is a *mammalogist*—a scientist who studies mammals—and he has been learning about whales for 10 years. In front of a full-scale, fiber glass model of a gigantic blue whale, Charles explained to Ben some of the reasons why whales are known to be mammals. On the blue whale's chin are a few bristly hairs—almost like whiskers. The humpback whale has these same kind of hairs coming out of the *tubercles* on its upper and lower jaws. Mammals are the only group of animals that have hair. Also, whales give birth to live young—they don't lay eggs like birds, reptiles, and fish do—and mother whales nurse their babies, just like all mammal mothers. Unlike fish, which filter oxygen through their gills, whales have nostrils and lungs, and must breathe air above the water.

Ben was more and more convinced. "Charlie," he said, "I understand a lot more about why whales are classified as mammals, but I still don't believe that their ancestors walked on land."

"Well," replied Charlie, "Dr. Frank Whitmore can tell you a lot more about that than I can. He's a *vertebrate paleontologist*, someone who studies the *fossil* remains of animals with backbones."

When Ben and Charlie arrived at Dr. Whitmore's office, they found him working on a fossil porpoise skull. Dr. Whitmore explained that the porpoise skull is 15 million years old, and that he'd recently dug it up in North Carolina. Like most paleontologists, Dr. Whitmore spends part of his time in a lab or office, and part of his time out in the field, finding and unearthing new fossils.

Dr. Whitmore has been studying whale evolution for many years. When Ben asked about the ancestors of whales, Dr. Whitmore said he had some proof that would convince Ben that whales' ancestors once walked on land.

Find out how a paleontologist works. Reconstruct the skeleton of a chicken, at home. The next time your family has chicken for dinner, collect the bones and scrape off any remaining meat. Remove the grease by boiling the bones in soapy water. (Get someone to help you with this part.) Sort out the cleaned, dry bones according to size and likeness. Then try to place the bones in their correct position in the skeleton. Start with the largest bone and fit smaller bones to it. When you find a fit, glue the bone in place, using white glue. From your reconstructed skeleton, draw some conclusions about the habits or behavior of the animal. For example, decide which behavior requires a large, hollow breastbone.

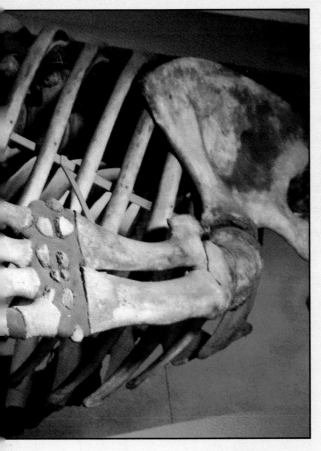

Ben got a close look at the skeleton of a modern gray whale. The picture on the far left shows the bones of the spinal column. The tiny pelvis is all that remains of land mammals' large pelvis and leg structure. The middle picture shows the rib cage and right flipper. The flippers have evolved from the arm of the whale's ancestors. Now the lengthened finger bones of the flippers help the whale paddle through water. The picture above shows the neck and jaw of the gray whale.

Dr. Whitmore showed Ben physical evidence that whales evolved from land mammals.

"We start off with the fact that they are mammals," said Dr. Whitmore. "We know that mammals appeared on the earth a long time back. The earliest specimens we have are about 200 million years old. So we take the modern whale, and use fossils to trace its ancestry back further and further into the past. And, as we trace whales back, we find that each fossil specimen looks a little bit like the one before it and a little bit like the one after it, but a little different, too. Finally, the oldest whale fossils begin to look a lot like land mammals."

"What are some of the differences you notice between modern whales and whale fossils?" Ben wanted to know.

Dr. Whitmore took Ben into a large room filled with shelves and shelves of fossilized whale bones. The fossils are millions of years old and have been collected from all over the world. "We study all different aspects of these bones," said Dr. Whitmore. "We may examine such things as the size and length of the snout. We also study the teeth— because they tell a lot about what the whale ate— and the position of the blowhole. The change in whales' blowholes, or nostrils, has been very dramatic."

"The whales I've seen have their blowholes right on top of their heads," said Ben.

"Just as all modern whales do," agreed Dr. Whitmore. He picked up the skull of a modern por-poise. And sure enough, Ben could see that the opening for its blowhole was right on top of its head. "Now let's go back 15 million years," said Dr. Whitmore, "almost no time to a paleontologist."

Ben and Dr. Whitmore looked at two different porpoise skulls, both 15 million years old. On both of them, the blowhole was right on top of the head, exactly where modern whales' blowholes are. But then Dr. Whitmore pointed out a 30-million-year-old skull that had come from the coast of Oregon. On this one, the blowhole was right in the middle of the snout, or rostrum. It was much farther forward than the blowholes in any of the other skulls. Not only that, but the nostril was pointing forward, rather than straight up like the others. "Somewhere between 15 and 30 million years ago, we know that something really big happened in the blowhole business," said Dr. Whitmore.

Then Dr. Whitmore showed Ben a skull that was still older—45 million years old. "Here's the tiny little braincase," said Dr. Whitmore, "which is small compared to modern whales. And where's the blowhole? Right out front at the end of the snout." Ben couldn't believe it. The older the whales, the farther forward their nostrils were. "Now let's go back again," Dr. Whitmore said, "to this 50-million-year-old skull. Until very recently, this was the oldest whale known."

"Its blowhole is at the very tip of its nose!"

"Right," said Dr. Whitmore. "If you found this

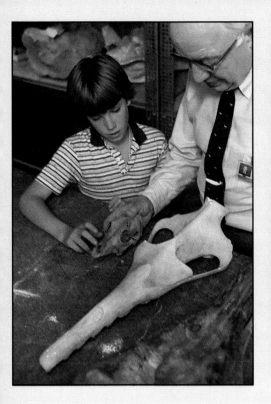

skull, what kind of animal would you think it was?"

Ben was stumped. He didn't think he'd recognize it as a whale.

"Does it resemble this?" Dr. Whitmore asked as he placed a very tiny skull next to the whale skull. The shapes of the two skulls were slightly different, but their nostrils were in the same place.

"Yes," said Ben, "it looks a lot like that."

"That," said Dr. Whitmore, "is the skull of a dog."

"A dog!" cried Ben. "You mean that the ancestors of whales were dogs?"

"No," said Dr. Whitmore. "But dogs and whales have a common ancestor—a mammal that walked on land. Many scientists share the theory that, at one time, food for land animals became scarce in some parts of the world. The whales' ancestors turned to the sea for their food. In order to become better at eating the food in the sea, their bodies slowly—over many many years—adapted to the water."

"Do creatures evolve just because they want to?" wondered Ben.

"No," said Dr. Whitmore, "although people used to think that was true. Now we know that evolution happens over a very long period of time. If you look at people, we all look a little different. That's because we all inherit different genes, some from our mothers, and some from our fathers. Over millions of years, these genes change. Sometimes

the change is good, sometimes bad, sometimes it doesn't matter. But if the change is good, if it helps the creature get along in the world, then that animal has an advantage over other animals. That animal and its offspring who inherit that genetic change are going to have a better chance at surviving. An example of this change is the whale's blowhole. The whales you saw last summer barely had to break the surface of the water to breathe. They could surface smoothly, breathe out and in, and quickly be on their way. Imagine the 50-million-year-old whale. It had to stop, stick its whole head and face out of the water, breathe, lower its head back down, and then take off to swim again. That wasn't very efficient for an animal that had to spend a lot of its time in water. So, over a period of time, the genetic changes that moved the blowhole back helped the animal to survive. Survival is the reason those changes got passed along. And that's how evolution happens—very slowly, in ways that help the animal."

"Dr. Whitmore," said Ben, "you've taught me a lot. You've actually given me proof that the ancestors of whales once walked on land, and I think I understand evolution now. I just have one more question. Am I evolving?"

"No," replied Dr. Whitmore. "You evolved from your ancestors, and your descendants will evolve from you. But you yourself are not evolving—you're just growing, a little older every day."

GOING FISHING

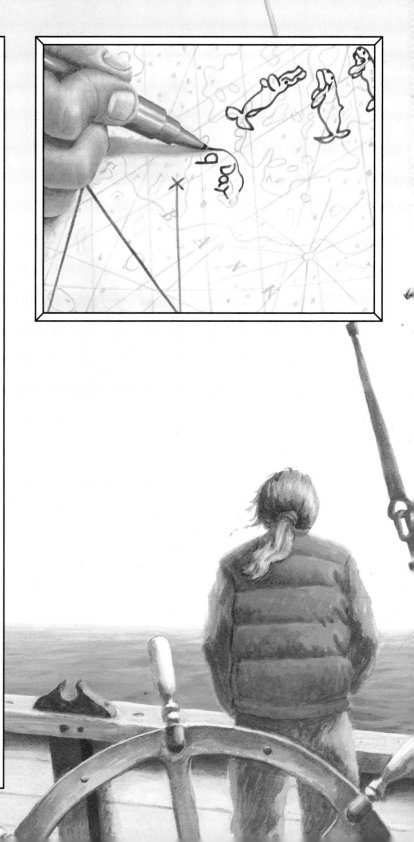

The days passed as the *Mimi* criss-crossed Georges Bank, and the whale census continued. There was plenty of other research work to do, also. The crew members identified individual whales by taking fluke photos and comparing them with those in the fluke catalogue. They collected and recorded data on whale behavior. They gathered information about the ocean in order to learn more about the whales' environment. When they weren't doing research, they were doing laundry, taking the helm, working in the galley. Whenever there was time, Ramon fished . . . and fished. But so far, all he had caught was seaweed.

Captain Granville gave C.T. a nautical chart identical to the one he used to chart and record the *Mimi*'s course. C.T. used the chart to keep his own record of the voyage.

After two weeks of data collection on Georges Bank, the *Mimi* headed northwest toward Rockland, Maine. Anne and Ramon had arranged to pick up some important research equipment. Also, it was time to replenish the supplies aboard the *Mimi*.

It was barely dawn on the day the *Mimi* was to dock at Rockland. Ramon awoke to find Arthur already dressed.

"What are you doing up so early?"

"I'm anxious, man," Arthur answered. "Anxious for port. Land. Civilization. People. Video games."

The first thing C.T. did that morning was update his chart. He checked the binnacle for the *Mimi*'s heading.

"How am I doing?" asked Captain Granville, who was at the helm.

"Right on course," C.T. confirmed. "Boy," he sighed, "everyone sure is itchy to get on land."

"Aren't you?" his grandfather asked.

"No. I kind of like it out here."

Captain Granville smiled at his grandson. "I know what you mean."

But Rockland was still several hours away, and there was work to be done before the *Mimi* put into port. C.T. sat down at the table in the saloon to work on his chart. Rachel was studying a book about whales, and Arthur was searching for something to eat.

"Zilch! Zip! Zero!" Arthur said. "There's nothing left to eat in this place."

"There's always peanut butter," Rachel pointed out.

"No," said Arthur, "I think it's a little too early for a dip in the mud bucket. We've gone through about twenty-five pounds of this stuff!" he moaned.

Rachel grimaced. "My mouth sticks together just thinking about it!"

"Ramon said he's going to catch fish for dinner," C.T. said optimistically.

"Ri-i-ight," Rachel said, not so sure.

Just then, Sally Ruth came in. "I've got a present for you, Arthur," she said, giving him a handful of fluke photos.

"Hey," said Arthur, looking through the photos, "**this** whale's not in the fluke catalogue." He grinned at Sally Ruth and handed Rachel a picture of a young man.

"Now **that** is a good-looking whale!" Rachel teased, just before Sally Ruth grabbed the picture away.

"That's the guy Sally Ruth can't wait to see again?" C.T. asked.

"Yep. That's Erik. He works with Ramon at the Institute," Rachel went on, "and he's meeting us in Rockland."

"Look at this, C.T.," Rachel said, pointing to a picture in her book. "That's a humpback eating. Its mouth is filled with fifteen or twenty tons of water and little fish."

"It looks all swollen!" C.T. said.

Arthur pointed to the ventral pleats of the humpback on the marine mammals chart. "Humpbacks have folds in their skin, C.T., so they can stretch their bodies like an accordion."

o they swallow all that water?" C.T. asked.

Rachel answered, "No, they strain the water through their *baleen*—these curtainlike things that hang down from the roofs of their mouths."

"Where are their teeth?" C.T. asked.

"Humpbacks don't have teeth," Rachel answered. "They use their tongues to push the water out through the baleen. The fish get trapped inside."

Arthur looked over at the echo sounder. "Hey, the water's getting shallower. We must be at Jeffreys Bank."

Rachel closed the book. "I have to take the water temperature," she said. C.T. offered to help her.

On deck, Ramon was fishing, and having no luck again. Exasperated, he stood up. "I give up! There isn't a fish within fifty kilometers of here."

Just then, Sally Ruth spotted something through her binoculars. "Look!" she shouted.

"Humpbacks?" Ramon asked.

"Yes," she confirmed. "And it looks like they're eating your fish."

Captain Granville suggested that they take a closer look at the whales.

"Let's go," Ramon said.

"What about my XBT readings?"

"Start them," Ramon answered. "This is a good chance to match water temperature with feeding behavior."

While the *Mimi* approached the whales, Rachel showed C.T. how an *eXpendable BathyThermograph*—XBT—works. She put the cylinder that contained the temperature sensor into the XBT launcher. Then she explained to C.T. how to remove the pin from the launcher and let the sensor drop into the water. As the sensor falls to the bottom, it reports the water temperatures through a cable connected to the computer.

While C.T. held the launcher, Rachel went below to get the computer ready. "Okay!" she called to C.T. He

pulled the pin from the launcher and the sensor dropped over the side. The thin copper wire attached to the sensor unwound from the launcher.

"I'll hold the launcher, C.T.," Sally Ruth offered. "You can go below and look at the graph on the computer."

On the computer screen, a line was appearing on the temperature/depth graph.

Rachel showed C.T. how to read the graph. "The horizontal line on the graph represents depth," she explained. "And the vertical line represents temperature. As the XBT sensor falls through the water, it reports the temperature to the computer through the copper wire. A line appears on the graph indicating what the temperature is at different depths. The line stops when the sensor hits bottom. Cold water is denser than warm water," she continued, "so cold water tends to sink to the bottom. That's why the temperature usually drops as the water gets deeper."

"Are you ready to do another one?" C.T. asked.

"Go ahead," Rachel answered.

On deck, C.T. asked Sally Ruth, "Do we just leave the XBT sensor on the ocean bottom?"

"Yes. That's why they're called expendable," Sally Ruth confirmed.

"Isn't that littering?" C.T. asked.

Anne overheard his question. "It bothers me too, C.T.," she said. "But I've come to believe that the information we get about the ocean from XBTs is worth that little bit of litter."

As the *Mimi* got closer to the whales, the crew could see a wide circle of bubbles forming on the ocean surface.

"What's that?" C.T. asked.

"A bubble cloud," Ramon answered.

"The whales seem to make the bubbles to stun the fish, or to make them group together more," Ramon explained.

"They're smart critters," the Captain noted. "What are they eating?"

"Sand lance," Ramon replied. "In other areas of the ocean they eat different kinds of fish, and little shrimplike creatures called *krill*."

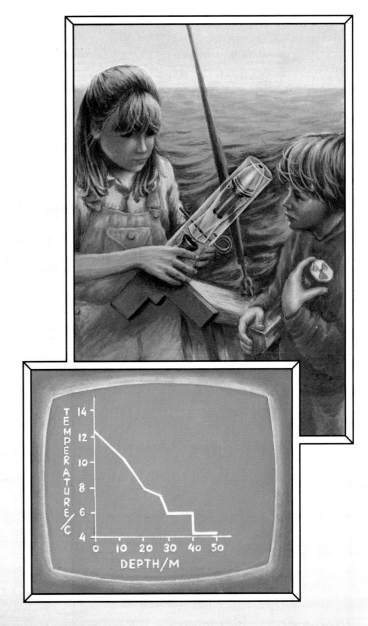

For a while longer the crew observed the feeding whales. Finally, it was time to head for port.

"By the way, Ramon," Anne said, "have you caught dinner yet?"

"Oh, uh, right. I was just about to," Ramon answered, picking up his fishing gear and heading for the stern.

The afternoon passed. The *Mimi* sailed toward Rockland. Once again, Ramon fished. Once again, he gave up and went below empty-handed.

"Hey, guys," Ramon said cheerfully, checking the galley shelves, "how about my specialty?"

"Rice and beans," Arthur, Anne, and Rachel moaned in unison.

"It's time for me to spell Sally Ruth at the helm," Arthur said.

"Hey, Arthur," Ramon asked, "would you do me a favor and stow my fishing gear? I left it up there."

On deck, when Arthur picked up the fishing rod the lure dropped into the water. As he started to reel it in, there was a tug on the line. Arthur stopped, unsure of what to do. There was another tug, and then another.

"Hang on, Arthur!" the Captain coached him.

"Ramon!" Arthur yelled, fighting to hold onto the rod against the powerful pull of whatever was at the end of the line. "Ramon, I've got a fish!"

An Appetite to Match

With a whale of an appetite, it isn't easy to eat your fill, especially if you eat some of the smallest plants and animals in the world.

The humpback whale eats algae, plankton, krill, and small fish. This living "soup" gets pretty thin when mixed with tons of ocean water. To make the soup richer and catch more fish, the humpback sometimes blows a bubble net. The whale swims up through the water in a spiral, blowing bubbles. The "net" of bubbles traps the food and forces it toward the surface. Then the humpback lunges upward through the bubble net with its mouth open. On the surface, the seawater strains through the two rows of baleen hanging like curtains from the whale's upper jaw. The whale pushes out all the extra water with its tongue, then swallows what's left.

How does baleen work? Try this experiment and see.

You will need

- a shallow pan – to represent the ocean bottom
- several cups of water – to represent the sea
- ½ teaspoon of very finely ground black pepper – to represent plankton
- a fine comb – to represent baleen

Steps

1. Fill pan with water to a depth of 2½ to 5 cm.
2. Sprinkle pepper into water, and mix well.
3. Try to "catch" specks of black pepper with your fingers.
4. Run the comb through the water to collect pepper (plankton).
5. Compare the two methods of collecting plankton. Which is faster and more efficient? Which would yield more pepper (plankton)? How would a bubble net help?

SCRAPING THE BOTTOM

*O*n board the *Mimi,* the crew members spend a lot of time looking at whales. They also spend a lot of time looking for whales to look at. And while gazing out at the sea, the crew thought about the other kinds of creatures that live in the ocean. These creatures range from microscopic plankton to fish weighing hundreds of pounds. There are more animals, and more kinds of animals, in the sea than there are on the land. Thousands of marine creatures have not even been named.

Compared to land animals, most marine animals have simple bodies. Over millions of years, most life in the sea has not evolved nearly as fast as life on land. While earthquakes, volcanoes, and floods have caused violent changes on land and to life on land, life in the sea has remained relatively stable. Most sea creatures, therefore, have simpler systems, and thus are easier to study. Their simpler systems make them good models for studying the more complex systems of human beings.

Horseshoe crabs, in existence for 500 million years, have hardly changed in the last 200 million years. Scientists at the Marine Biological Laboratory have discovered that their blood can be used to detect endotoxins, which are poisonous substances found in the blood of people with certain diseases.

One of the most famous places in the world for the study of marine animals is the Marine Biological Laboratory (MBL) in Woods Hole, Massachusetts. Established in 1888, MBL is ideally located on the "elbow" of Cape Cod. Marshes, a rocky shore, large bays and inlets, and deep water all are close by. The cold Labrador Current from the north and the warm Gulf Stream from the south meet near Woods Hole. As a result, a huge variety of ocean animals lives in this area.

Scientists at MBL study marine animals not so much to learn about them, as to learn more about humans. Some research laboratories use rats, mice and guinea pigs for this purpose. At MBL, scientists use clams, squid, and crabs to learn more about such processes as how nerves work, how our cells divide, and how our bodies fight disease. A great deal of knowledge about how we can fight human illnesses has come from the Woods Hole Marine Biological Laboratory.

Each year MBL scientists use 75,000 animals of 250 different species for their research. How do they get all these animals? The Lab employs eight collectors. They are fishermen/naturalists who know where specific sea animals live, how to catch them, and how to bring them back alive. John Valois is the chief collector. Mary Tanner, who plays Rachel, visited him one autumn day to find out more about his work.

John thought the best way to introduce Mary to his work would be to let her spend a day with him. First they visited the supply department where the collected animals are held until needed. Mary got a chance to see and touch creatures such as sea robins, squid, horseshoe crabs, skates, starfish, and dogfish.

But what Mary really wanted to do was go out to sea. So she and John soon boarded the research vessel *Gemma* for a collecting trip. John had an order for some sea urchins, and he also wanted to show Mary a variety of marine environments. An environment often determines the appearance and behavior of the animals that live in it. This phenomenon is called *adaptation,* and can be seen in such results as the shape, coloration, and feeding habits of animals.

At MBL, scientists use clams, squid, and crabs to learn more about such processes as how our nerves work, how our cells divide, and how our bodies fight disease. Here, John Valois shows Mary how to hold a spider crab.

To collect sea animals, Mary and the Gemma's crew used a naturalist's dredge—a big, metal net that is dragged along the ocean bottom.

In which environment are these animals likely to be found?

With their tube feet and prickly spines, sea urchins are well adapted to a rocky underwater environment.

To collect the animals, John and Mary brought along a naturalist's dredge—a big metal net that can be dragged along the ocean bottom. They planned to sample three different environments that day. Their first stop was an area of the ocean with a sandy bottom.

A sandy bottom is a very unstable environment because ocean currents can shift the sand easily. So, most of the animals that live there had to develop special ways of staying put. Some do this by burrowing under the sand. Others use the sand to construct a stable place to live. For example, the sand sponge, a large colony of very tiny animals, builds a home out of sand and mucous. Alone, these animals would be rather insignificant, and would drift about. But together they form a large, stable structure fit for life in a sandy environment.

John and Mary next went to a spot with a rocky bottom. Animals that live among rocks have a fairly tough structure. They have to be able to hold onto the rocks so they can steady themselves or move around without getting injured. Crabs, lobsters, starfish, and sea urchins all live among rock and gravel. John lowered the dredge to the bottom and collected some of these animals. He showed Mary the sea urchin's tube feet: the little suction cups it uses to stay on a rock. They put a number of urchins into a bucket to take back to the laboratory.

Mary piloted the boat to the last stop of the day, Hadley's Harbor, which is famous for its muddy bottom. A muddy bottom is found only where trees and bushes grow near the water. The mud is formed from leaves falling into the water and decaying, over a period of many years. The mud they hauled up on deck looked and smelled disgusting. John explained that the smell was caused by hydrogen sulphide, a gas formed naturally by the process of decay.

Tube worms and some kinds of shellfish are the chief inhabitants of a muddy environment. Mary and John found a couple of mollusks with delicate shells. These animals are able to survive without tough, thick shells because they are cushioned by the soft mud. They also found an unusual worm called a beak thrower. The beak thrower moves through the mud by shooting its *proboscis,* or beak, out in front of it and dragging the rest of its body behind.

On the way back to Woods Hole, Mary thought that collecting was a fun job. John got to spend his days on a boat. Also, he combined the knowledge of a scientist with the skills of a fisherman.

Imagine that you, like Mary Tanner, get a chance to visit the MBL supply department where marine animals are held. On this day, too many animals have been collected, so the Lab wants to return some to the ocean. Because you've read "Scraping the Bottom," you offer to help. You are handed some buckets and asked to collect rocky bottom dwellers from the Lab. Which animals should go into your collecting buckets? Read these animal descriptions and decide:

1. has soft body, hard shell, and a single foot for digging
2. spins tough, ropelike strands for anchoring
3. has no eyes; has pointed foot for burrowing
4. has muscular foot that can withstand pull of 400 pounds
5. has soft, stout, round body; tunnels into the bottom

"**H**ey, Ramon! Arthur's got a fish!" C.T. leaned over the side of the *Mimi*, eager to catch a glimpse of Arthur's catch.

Arthur was more surprised than anyone. Sally Ruth, the Captain, and C.T. shouted encouragement as he struggled to reel in the fish.

Ramon arrived just as Arthur swung the wriggling fish onto the deck.

"What is it!" Sally Ruth asked.

"It's a shark!" Ramon said. "That's great!"

"A SHARK!" exclaimed Arthur and C.T., backing away.

Ramon grasped the fish firmly behind the head and held it up. "No, it's okay, you guys," he said. "It's edible. In fact, around here they call it a dogfish."

Arthur, Sally Ruth, and C.T. came closer.

"Look, feel," Ramon encouraged them. "It doesn't have scales like other fish. Its body is covered with little teeth called *denticles*."

Cautiously, the others touched the shark.

"Awesome!" said Arthur.

"Its skin is really rough," Sally Ruth said.

Ramon looked admiringly at the shark. "It's a nice one, too," he said, turning to Arthur. "How did you **do** that?"

Arthur still couldn't believe what he had done. "I was picking up your gear, and the thing on the end—the lure—fell overboard. Next thing I knew, POW! It took off, and Captain Granville told me to hold on."

"Yeah," C.T. added excitedly, "it looked like the rod would break!"

Ramon looked at the shark again. "It really put up a fight, huh?" he said wistfully. All that time fishing with no luck. And now Arthur, who had **never** been fishing, caught their dinner—without even trying!

"It was kind of fun," Arthur said. "Maybe I'll borrow your fishing stuff sometime."

Ramon laughed weakly and tossed the shark into the cooler. They were nearing Rockland, and it was time to get back to work.

C.T. updated his chart. On their fifteenth day out of Gloucester, they were heading for port again. Soon they would dock at Rockland, Maine, to pick up supplies. There they would also meet Erik, who was bringing them an important piece of research equipment.

When the *Mimi* motored into the harbor, Erik was on the dock to greet them.

"Excited?" Anne asked Sally Ruth.

Sally Ruth nodded and quickly added, "This is crazy! We only knew each other for one month!"

"That's your boyfriend?" C.T. asked sullenly.

"Just a friend," Sally Ruth replied.

"Sure," said C.T.

Now Erik waved and signed: Welcome to land. Great to see you again.

Once the *Mimi* was securely tied up at the dock, Erik came aboard.

"You learned sign!" Sally Ruth said, obviously pleased.

"I'm **learning** sign," said Erik with a grin.

"Hey, Erik! *¿Qué pasa?*" Ramon greeted him.

"Ramon!" The two friends shook hands. Turning to Anne, Erik said, "You must be Dr. Abrams. It's a pleasure to meet you. I've heard a lot about you and read all your papers."

"Call me Anne," she said, and introduced Erik to the others.

"Care to join us for dinner?" Arthur asked. "Here's the menu," he said, opening the cooler.

"There's plenty of it," Anne added. "Fresh caught just an hour ago," said Ramon.

Erik was impressed. "Ramon! We were at sea for three months last summer, and I never saw you catch anything but seaweed."

Realizing Erik's mistake, Ramon protested, "Actually, I didn't . . ."

But Arthur interrupted. "He's even teaching me to fish," he said to Erik.

Over dinner, Erik proposed a toast: "To the great provider—the sea," he said, raising his glass. "And to Ramon, who reaped the harvest."

Once again Ramon tried to correct Erik's mistaken impression that it was he who had caught the shark.

And once again Arthur interrupted. "What's for dessert?"

"Hey, Erik," Rachel said. "Didn't you say something earlier about a surprise?"

The surprise was a film. Erik had made it the winter before on a research expedition aboard the *Regina Maris*. That was how he and Sally Ruth had met.

They set up the projector on the dock and used a sail for a screen. Captain Granville even found some popcorn in the galley.

"That's the *Regina Maris*," Erik said when the film began and a beautiful sailing ship appeared on the makeshift screen.

"So what's *Regina Maris*?" Arthur asked, "Latin for 'love boat'?"

Captain Granville laughed with the others. "It means 'queen of the sea,'" he explained.

"Anyhow," Erik continued, "the *Regina Maris* sort of follows the humpbacks. She goes to the Caribbean in the winter and spends the summer in the North Atlantic."

When the film showed a whale breaching, Rachel asked, "So the whales we've been seeing up here in the Gulf of Maine were down there in the Caribbean last winter?"

"Most likely," Erik confirmed.

Now the film showed a man in the *crow's nest* of the *Regina Maris*. "Who's that?" C.T. asked.

"The captain, George Nichols. He's an old friend of mine," Captain Granville said.

"What's he doing up there?" C.T. asked.

Erik answered, "He's on the lookout to make sure we don't bump into coral reefs and damage the ship. We spent most of our time on this shallow bank called Silver Bank. It's very near the Dominican Republic. That's where the humpbacks from the western North Atlantic go in the winter to mate and have their babies."

In the film, Sally Ruth and another person were matching fluke photographs.

"That's Ken Balcomb," Sally Ruth said.

"He's the chief scientist," Erik continued. "By matching up these flukes, scientists can chart the migration of the whales to and from the Caribbean."

"We haven't seen you yet, Erik," Rachel observed.

"That's because I'm taking the pictures."

"No wonder Sally Ruth is in every shot," said Rachel.

The film continued, showing the crew of the *Regina Maris* doing the same kind of work the crew of the *Mimi* did. That work included everything from taking a whale census, observing and recording whale behavior, and matching flukes, to raising sails and cooking dinner.

"Oh, this is the best part," Sally Ruth said. On the screen, she and Ken Balcomb were in a rubber dinghy. They put on snorkeling gear and jumped into the water. "Wait 'til you see this," Sally Ruth said to the *Mimi* crew. "Did you record the sound?" she asked Erik.

Now Sally Ruth and Ken were swimming underwater. Only a few feet away from them were several humpback whales.

"Wow!" C.T. exclaimed. "You were in the water, right next to them!"

Suddenly, an eerie and beautiful sound filled the air.

"Holy cow!" said Rachel.

"What is that?" Arthur asked.

Ramon answered, "It's whale song."

"Wait a minute," Rachel said suddenly, turning toward Sally Ruth. "How did you hear whale song?"

"I couldn't hear it," Sally Ruth answered, "but I could feel it on my chest. I didn't know what it was until later, when Ken explained what I felt."

Ken had shown Sally Ruth a voiceprint of whale song. The sounds the humpbacks make have distinctive patterns. That's why they're called songs. At any given time, all the humpbacks in a herd are following the same pattern in the sounds they make—they're all singing the same song. By recording the songs with underwater microphones, it's possible to make voiceprints and actually see the patterns. In the film, Ken pointed to one of the marks on the voiceprint. He explained that the mark represented a sound kind of like a roar. When seen on a machine that shows the wavelengths of sounds, the whale roar has a very long wavelength. The

long wavelength is what made it possible for Sally Ruth to feel the vibrations of the sound so strongly.

"Underwater you can hear the whales for miles," Erik added. "The water is always filled with sound. As far as we know, only the males sing."

Rachel asked, "And they only sing when they're in the Caribbean?"

"Right."

On the screen, two more whales—a calf and its mother—swam gracefully in the clear Caribbean water.

"How old is that calf?" Anne asked.

"Probably only a few weeks," said Erik. "They're thirteen to fifteen feet long and weigh a ton and a half at birth. They grow about one and a half feet a month."

"Weren't you scared to be so close to them?" Rachel asked.

"A little at first," Sally Ruth answered, "but they were so gentle. That's when I got hooked on whales forever."

When the film ended, there were cheers from the group. They turned to thank Erik, but he was gone. So was Sally Ruth. The others were puzzled until they looked toward the stern of the Mimi. There they saw Sally Ruth and Erik watching the moon as it traced a silvery path on the surface of the dark, calm water.

"And they lived happily ever after. THE END," Rachel said dramatically.

"Oh, barf!" added C.T.

69

That's Some Baby!

Human babies and whale calves are a lot alike. Both have lungs and breathe air. Both are born live, instead of hatched from eggs. And both can drink milk from their mothers! But look at these differences!

An average human newborn gains about 30 grams a day, or about 210 grams a week. It doubles its birth weight in about 6 months.

Scientists estimate that an average blue whale calf gains 120 kg per day, or about 5 kg per hour. It doubles its birth weight in about 7 days.

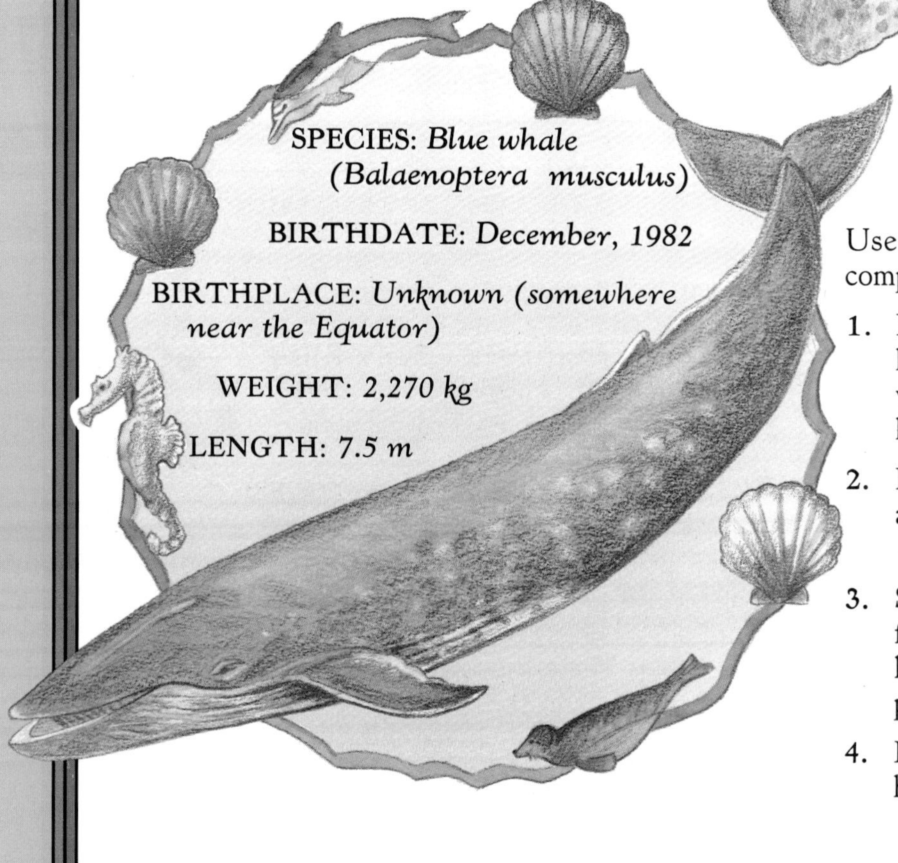

SPECIES: *Human being (Homo sapiens)*

BIRTHDATE: *June 13, 1982*

BIRTHPLACE: *New York, New York*

WEIGHT: *3 kg*

LENGTH: *51 cm*

SPECIES: *Blue whale (Balaenoptera musculus)*

BIRTHDATE: *December, 1982*

BIRTHPLACE: *Unknown (somewhere near the Equator)*

WEIGHT: *2,270 kg*

LENGTH: *7.5 m*

Use the information above to make these comparisons:

1. How long would it take an average human baby to gain the same amount of weight a blue whale calf gains in one hour? (Note: 1 kg = 1,000 g)

2. How many times longer is a blue whale at birth than a human baby? (Note: 1m = 100 cm)

3. Suppose human babies kept growing as fast as they do in their first 6 months of life. How much would you weigh at your present age?

4. In what other ways can you compare human babies and blue whale calves?

Thinking About Baby Whales

A baby whale is come
Seeks through the world
And finds a home
What beautiful is born.

William Lopez, age 10

The poem and picture celebrate the birth of a
baby whale. Imagine what it would be like to
see a whale calf that has just been born.
Create your own poem or picture to
welcome the newcomer.

Poem, "A Baby Whale is Come," reprinted from *There's a
Sound in the Sea: A Child's Eye View of the Whale*, collected
by Tamar Griggs. Copyright ©1975 by Tamar Griggs.
Reprinted by permission.

SONGS IN THE SEA

Humback whales follow the best climate, year round. In summer, they swim to cool waters – such as the Gulf of Maine or the Southern Atlantic east of Argentina – where they feed all season. In winter, they swim to warm tropical waters where they mate and give birth. In tropical waters some humpbacks show a unique behavior – they sing. That is, they make a series of unusual sounds that fall into a pattern.

Other whales make sounds, but none as elaborate as the sounds made by humpback whales. All summer long humpbacks are fairly quiet. But when winter comes and it is time to leave for warmer waters, they start producing their elaborate sounds.

People who study humpback whales believe that only the males sing. The reason whales sing is unknown, but there are many theories. It may be territorial – one whale telling all the others that this is his space. It may be a mating call – the male is telling the females that he is available. It may even be an expression of pleasure or contentment – a form of play. Or perhaps it is a combination of these things. No one knows for sure.

Nor does anyone quite understand how the humpbacks make their elaborate sounds. No air comes out of their mouths or blowholes when they sing, and they don't have typical vocal cords. Some scientists think that the whales have an air-filled chamber in their throats that they can open and

Mark Graham likes new wave music. Since visiting Katy Payne, he likes "whale wave" as well.

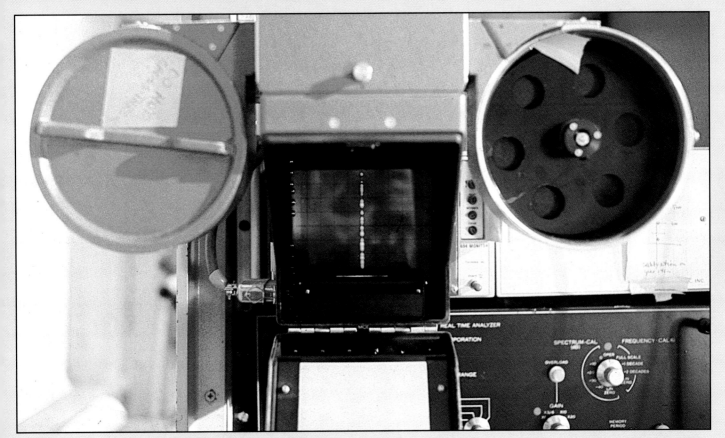

A spectrum analyzer translates sound into a visual image.

close. They think there might be a membrane stretched across that air chamber that can be loosened or tightened as the air moves back and forth. This would be a little bit like a bagpipe. In a bagpipe, air is pushed through different parts of the instrument to make different sounds.

Mark Graham, who plays Arthur in "The Voyage of the *Mimi*," is a big music fan. Intrigued by these singing whales, he wanted to learn more about their sounds. So, he visited Katy Payne at her studio workshop in a barn in northern Massachusetts.

For 17 years, Katy Payne, with her husband Roger Payne, has been studying humpback whales and the sounds they make. She has spent many winters on a boat, listening to and recording the songs of whales. Katy began her work by dropping a *hydrophone,* an underwater microphone, into the water where she knows there are humpbacks. She usually works near the islands of Hawaii, Bermuda, or Socorro. The sounds picked up by the hydrophone are recorded on tape. Many people have recognized the beauty of the sounds whales make. But it was Roger Payne who first discovered that the sounds have regular patterns. It is because of these patterns that the sounds are called songs.

Birds and frogs are other animals that are known to sing. Their sounds fall into patterns, but most of the patterns are quite simple. For example, a bird sings "chick-a-dee-dee-dee." It then repeats that sim-

ple pattern. But a whale's song is more complex and can last longer. One humpback song may last anywhere from five minutes to half an hour.

How does Katy Payne find the pattern? It is too difficult to find just by listening. So she uses a machine called a *spectrum analyzer* to help her. A spectrum analyzer translates sound into a visual image. When sound is played into a spectrum analyzer, a light pattern appears on the screen. The pattern changes as the sound changes. It becomes darker or lighter as the sound gets louder or softer. It jumps up if the pitch is high and sinks down if the pitch is low. The spectrum analyzer takes a continuous photo of the light pattern as it changes on the screen. This photo comes out on a long strip of paper called a spectrogram.

To show Mark how the machine works, Katy played a song tape into the spectrum analyzer. The markings on the paper that came out were the "notes" of the whale song. Katy showed Mark how to read the spectrogram, and together they "sang" the notes. Katy and Mark sounded a little like whales.

A humpback whale breaching.

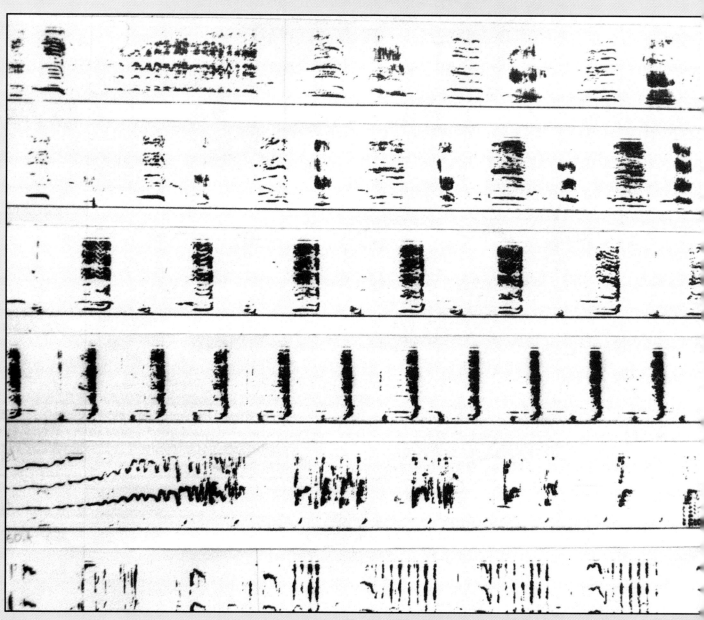

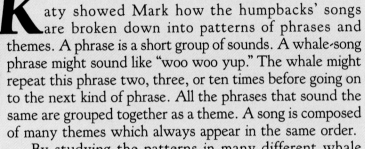

The sounds of whales are pictured in these spectrograms. Groans, moans, yups, chirps, woos, and grunts are just some of the sounds found in whale songs. Probably no one in the world knows these songs better than Katy Payne.

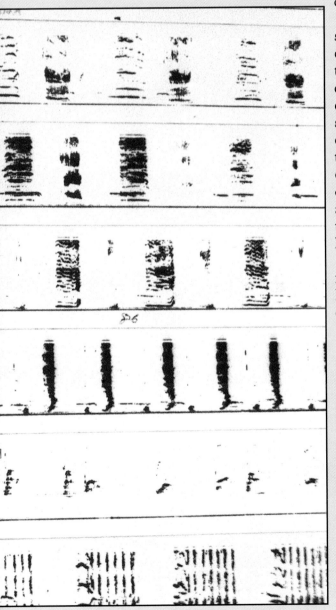

Katy showed Mark how the humpbacks' songs are broken down into patterns of phrases and themes. A phrase is a short group of sounds. A whale-song phrase might sound like "woo woo yup." The whale might repeat this phrase two, three, or ten times before going on to the next kind of phrase. All the phrases that sound the same are grouped together as a theme. A song is composed of many themes which always appear in the same order.

By studying the patterns in many different whale songs, Katy made a startling discovery, in 1969. She discovered that the song of the humpback changes all the time. At the beginning of winter, all the singers in one area of the ocean start out singing last winter's song. But by the end of the winter, their song is very different. And all the singers have learned the new song! How does a humpback do it? Nobody knows. Perhaps one whale changes the pattern and the others copy him. Or perhaps all the singers try different sounds here and there and the changes are accepted by the group. These changes happen every year, and are special to humpbacks. No other animals are known to change their songs in this way. As Katy Payne says, humpback whales are composers.

When he left Katy's studio, Mark was carrying a gift from Katy. It was a recording of that season's whale song. For Mark, a tape of humpback whale song adds a new dimension to his music collection.

Find out why your favorite song is called a song. Listen to it played on the radio or television or on your own stereo, and see if you can hear patterns. Try to pick out the patterns of the music, not the words. When you think you've found the patterns, devise a way to write down the sounds that are the same and the sounds that are different. For example, use lines—curved, straight, and jagged—or use simple word phrases—"tra la la" and "dum de dum."

Were you able to find patterns in the song just by listening? Is there anything that would have made your job easier?

FASTENING ON

When Erik arrived at the *Mimi* the next morning, Anne and Ramon were having coffee on deck.

"Where is everyone?" Erik called from the dock.

"Captain Granville took Rachel, Arthur, and C.T. to the whaling museum," Ramon answered.

"And Sally Ruth just got up," Anne added. "You guys must have painted the town red last night!"

Just then Sally Ruth came up on deck carrying the coffee pot. "Good morning!" she called to Erik.

"Good morning!" Erik called.

"Did you bring the radio tag?" Ramon asked Erik.

"Sure did," he replied. "All you need now is a whale to stick it on!"

Meanwhile, at the whaling museum, Captain Granville, C.T., Arthur, and Rachel were learning about the history of whaling.

C.T. and his grandfather were examining a model of an old whaling ship. "This is the *Alice Mandel*," Captain Granville said, "the vessel Nelson Granville sailed on. He was your great-great-grandfather, the one who wrote the journal. He was a harpooner."

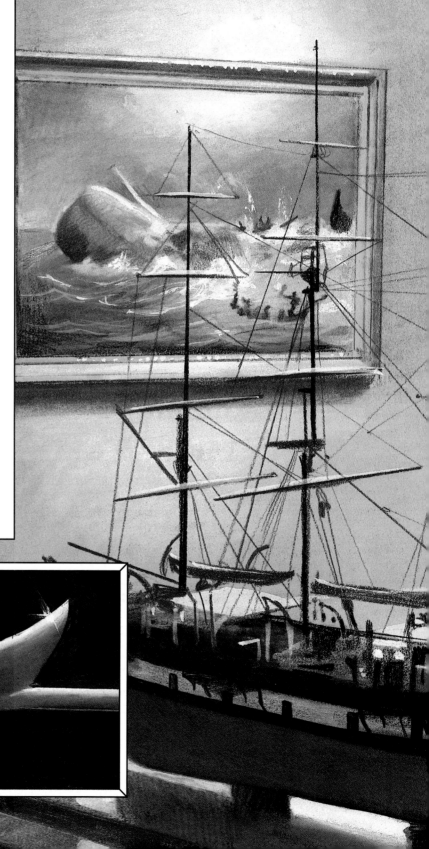

They moved on to an exhibit that included an actual harpoon from Nelson Granville's time.

"This is called a toggle-head harpoon," the Captain explained. "The harpoon itself was attached to the chase boat by a heavy rope. When it went into the whale, the barbed end would turn up, so the harpoon couldn't come out. Sometimes, in an effort to get away, the whale would tow the boat for hours."

"I don't understand why the harpoon didn't kill the whale," C.T. said.

"First of all, it didn't go deep enough," his grandfather explained. "And second, the whale is a big and powerful animal."

"Then what did they kill the whale with?" C.T. wanted to know.

Captain Granville pointed to several long, sharp-tipped iron lances. "When the whale finally got so tired it couldn't swim any more, the whalers pulled the boat alongside it. Then they drove one of those lances into the whale's lungs. That's what killed the whale."

C.T. frowned. "Poor whale."

"It wasn't any fun for the whalemen, either," his grandfather pointed out.

The next stop in the museum was at the theater that showed films of both old and modern methods of hunting whales. The group found out that the many-sailed whaling vessels with their small chase boats of the old days have been replaced in modern times by efficient, seagoing "factory" ships. Airplanes are used to locate whales. Hand-thrown harpoons and lances have been replaced by powerful harpoons fired from cannons in the bows of fast, motor-powered chase boats. When it enters the whale's body, the massive steel head of the modern harpoon explodes. And death comes quickly.

The bloody scenes of modern whalers cutting up the carcass of a whale were finally too much for Rachel and Arthur. They slipped out of the museum theater before the film was over.

Back at the *Mimi*, Anne, Ramon, and Sally Ruth were learning about the suction-cup whale tag Erik had designed.

"It's similar to the whale tag now in use," Erik explained. "The big difference is that this tag sticks to the surface of the skin. It is like a big suction cup on a dart. My tag doesn't penetrate the skin as the other tag is designed to do."

Anne and Sally Ruth examined Erik's tag closely. "The *transmitter* is in the cylinder?" Anne asked.

"Right," Erik said. "The transmitter sends out a radio signal. The *receiver* picks up the signal when the whale is on the surface."

"Sometimes in heavy seas the signal is lost because of the waves, even when the whale is on the surface," Ramon added.

Erik then explained how the tag would be shot onto the whale with a crossbow, and Sally Ruth tried it out. It worked. The tag hit the back of Erik's truck and stuck there. Then they all tested the transmitter and receiver to make sure both parts were working properly.

When the others returned from the whaling museum, they, too, were eager to learn about the whale tag, until they saw the crossbow. Images of harpoons, lances, and butchered whales were still fresh in their minds.

"My friend Wendell's father hunts deer with a crossbow," C.T. said. "The arrow goes right through the deer's body."

"Well, we're not going to shoot a whale," Ramon tried to reassure him.

"You mean we're not going to shoot an arrow," Rachel corrected emphatically. "But we sure as heck are planning to shoot a whale."

Arthur nodded in agreement with Rachel's criticism. "Some of that stuff we just saw in the museum was pretty disgusting," he said. "It seems humans have messed with whales enough."

Anne and Ramon responded to the kids' concerns.

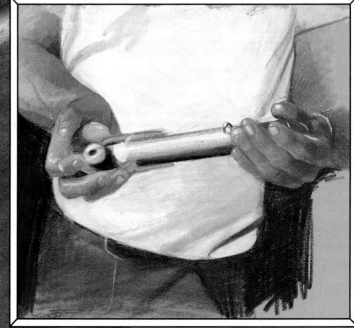

"It's only a suction cup," Ramon said. "Although we can't be sure it doesn't hurt, we do know whales react more to loud noises than they do to this tag."

"Suppose you hit the whale in the blowhole?" Rachel wondered.

Anne answered, "That's something we will have to be very careful about."

The young people still seemed skeptical.

"Look," Ramon went on, "I would never knowingly hurt a whale. We care a lot about these animals. That's why we study them. We've thought a lot about the use of the radio tag."

"If the tag works properly," Anne continued, "we will be able to gather information about the whale without actually seeing it. That means we'll be observing a whale that doesn't know it's being observed. The knowledge we gain about its movements and daily cycle will help us protect whales better," she concluded.

Sally Ruth added, "I wouldn't help with the tagging if I thought it would hurt the whale."

Gradually, Rachel, Arthur, and C.T. became convinced that the tagging could benefit whales.

The discussion had ended when Captain Granville joined the group.

"Looks good for tomorrow, folks. The dock master tells me several humpbacks have been sighted on Grumpy Ledge," he reported.

"That's not very far from here," Sally Ruth noted.

Ramon was eager to try out the tag. "Why don't we go this afternoon?"

"We still have supplies to pick up," Captain Granville said.

"We have enough supplies on board for four or five days," Anne pointed out. "The tag won't stay attached for that long. And if we don't tag a whale today, we can come back in for the rest of the supplies."

"It's okay by me," the Captain agreed. "You're the boss."

"I wish I had time to go with you," Erik told Sally Ruth. "Call when you get back."

They kissed goodbye. "Take care," Sally Ruth said quietly.

The *Mimi* was soon under way again. And the dock master had been right. At Grumpy Ledge the crew sighted humpbacks.

Quickly, Anne and Ramon climbed into the inflatable boat they had borrowed in Rockland. Anne ran the outboard motor as Ramon prepared the crossbow and tag. The inflatable approached a pair of humpbacks. They appeared to be a mother and her calf. Anne maneuvered the boat carefully. Ramon chose his target, steadied himself in the boat, took careful aim,

and fired! The tag sailed through the air and landed solidly on the large back of the larger whale. Cheers rose from the *Mimi.*

The whale seemed unaware of the suction-cup tag, and, with her calf, lolled about on the surface nearby for several minutes. Finally, the two whales arched their sleek backs, dove gracefully, and disappeared from sight.

Anne and Ramon returned to the *Mimi.* The crew members prepared to follow the tagged whale's radio signal. But where would it lead them?

Aware or Unaware— Does it Matter?

Anne and Ramon argue in favor of using Erik's radio tag. Ramon claims the tag won't hurt a whale if it's used properly. Anne points out that it will enable the crew to gather information about a whale that doesn't know it's being observed. Do subjects—human or animal—behave differently when they are aware of being watched? Try these experiments, and form your own conclusions.

Phase I

1. Choose a classmate as a subject.
2. Do not inform your subject that you are observing him or her as part of an experiment.
3. Choose a setting and a situation easy to use again. For example, choose the halls where you know your subject hangs out at certain times of the day, or the library, the gym, a playground, or the school bus.
4. Observe your subject for a period of five minutes.
5. Keep a written record of your subject's actions and mannerisms by answering these questions:
   - What is the subject doing? Describe the action.
   - What or whom is the subject looking at?
   - Does the subject speak? To whom? How often?
   - What expressions do you observe on the subject's face?

Record all actions, expressions, and mannerisms you observe.

Phase II

1. Repeat the experiment in the same setting and situation.
2. This time, inform your subject that you intend to observe him or her for five minutes as part of a scientific experiment.
3. Do not reveal what you observed in Phase I.
4. Repeat Phase I steps 4 and 5.

Observations

Compare the observations you made in Phase I and Phase II by answering these questions:

1. Did your subject's behavior change? How? List details.
2. Are there factors, or variables, that affected your subject's behavior? (For example: time of day, weather, number of people in area.)
3. Why do you think your subject's behavior changed?
4. How does awareness of being observed affect behavior?

HANDS FULL OF WORDS

Gallaudet College is the only liberal arts college for the deaf in the world.

While filming "The Voyage of the *Mimi*," Mary Tanner, who plays Rachel, and Judy Pratt, who plays Sally Ruth, became friends. Recently, Mary visited Judy at her school, Gallaudet College in Washington, D.C. All the students at Gallaudet are deaf, and Mary wanted to learn more about how deaf people communicate.

In the cafeteria, Mary was bewildered. How would she ever find Judy? There were many students there, all using a language Mary didn't understand. At last, Judy found *her*.

After lunch and before going to Judy's classes, they stopped off at the audiology lab. Judy had to have her hearing tested.

The staff at the Gallaudet audiology lab studies the ways people hear. Their findings help hearing-impaired people perceive more sounds and speak more clearly.

Lisa Holden Pitt, a psychologist, led Judy to a soundproof room and gave her headphones. From the control room, Lisa sent Judy a series of sound signals through the headphones. The first sounds were very low in pitch, and then they got higher and higher in pitch. All the sounds started out loud and then got softer. When she could hear a sound, Judy pressed a button. When the button was pressed, a mechanical pen made a mark on a graph.

Later, Lisa explained the graph to Judy and Mary: Judy heard only the sounds that were lowest in pitch. This probably means that Judy hears male voices, which are lower in pitch, better than female voices. The "s" and "sh" sounds are hardest for Judy to hear. Because she can't hear those sounds, she finds them hard to pronounce. Judy confirmed Lisa's findings.

Then Lisa tested Mary's hearing. The results were dramatically different. It was easy for Mary to hear even the highest-pitched tones that Lisa sent her through the headphones. The testing session made Mary realize the extent of Judy's deafness and appreciate how well Judy speaks.

Judy and Mary spent the rest of the afternoon attending classes.

After a long school day, Mary and Judy relaxed in the dorm with Judy's roommates. Mary described her day at Gallaudet. She said she felt like a visitor to a world in which she didn't belong and didn't understand everything that went on.

Judy said that was how she had felt during the filming of "The Voyage of the *Mimi*."

"Last summer, I was the only deaf person in the show. Sometimes it's hard to express how I feel in oral communication, especially when there's a big group of people. It's hard for me to keep up with the conversation when a lot of people are talking.

"So, once in a while, if there's a party or something, I don't feel it's worth going because I know I won't keep up with what's happening. If other people are laughing, I may laugh too. But do I always understand? No.

"I don't want to just sit back and watch and make other people wonder what's wrong. I don't want anyone to feel pity for me or think, 'She's lonely.' I don't like that."

All the facilities and programs are carefully planned for the deaf and hearing impaired. In the picture on the preceding page, Lisa Holden Pitt and Mary Tanner are shown in the audiology lab. Judy had her hearing tested in this lab. Like most deaf people, Judy can hear some sounds.

Loss of one or more of the senses restricts, but does not always prevent, communication. Find out for yourself. You need an audience—one person will do—to try these:

1. Describe a spiral staircase without using your hands and without referring to the term.
2. Read a short paragraph using only your voice and *not* moving your lips, tongue, and teeth.
3. Tell a three-sentence story by means of charades.

Did you succeed at all times in communicating with the other person or persons? With which activity did you have the most success? the least success? How do you know?

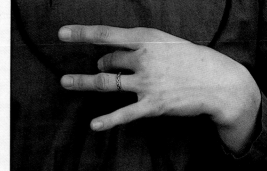

I   *like*

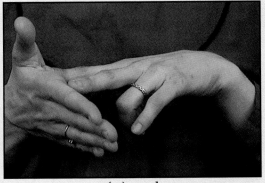

(to) read

books.

The next day at the library, Judy and Mary met a woman named Janice Adams. Janice is blind as well as deaf, so she can't see sign language. But she can feel sign language by putting her hand on top of the hand of her interpreter, Leah Subak. Leah describes what she hears and sees, and Janice understands through touch.

Janice was born deaf, and slowly lost her sight between the ages of 15 and 20. Not long ago, she married a hearing, seeing man. On their honeymoon, they rode a bicycle-built-for-two 150 miles through Vermont.

Janice reads braille and enjoys reading and cooking. It surprised Mary to learn that Janice also plays the piano and is able to enjoy music. Like most deaf people, she feels the vibrations when she is touching the source of the sound – such as a piano – or when the sound is loud enough.

In fact, that's how the Gallaudet football team communicates during a game. When a member of the team on the sidelines hits a big bass drum, the players on the field feel the vibrations and know when to start a play. Judy told Mary that the huddle – players clustering together to plan the next play – was invented at Gallaudet. In a huddle, the players were able to keep the other team from seeing their sign language.

Before Mary left, Judy gave her a book about sign language. Mary said she would learn some signs before she visited Gallaudet again. When she came back, she, too, could have "hands full of words."

TRACKING THE WHALE

The humpback swam along with the radio tag affixed to her back. Under full sail, the *Mimi* tracked her by following the signal transmitted by the tag. Whenever possible, the crew members observed the whale and her calf and recorded their observations.

"There!" cried Sally Ruth, as the whale broke the surface of the water.

"Can you see the radio tag?" C.T. asked.

"Yep," Rachel answered. When the whale arched her sleek back to dive, the red and white tag was clearly visible. "It's our whale, all right."

"The suction cup has slipped back a little," Arthur pointed out. "It's just behind the dorsal fin now."

Below deck, Anne and Ramon checked the radio tag *automatic direction finder*.

"It's still working," Anne said.

"I think the tag's on good and tight," Ramon replied.

"Congratulations, Ramon," Anne said, reaching across the table to shake his hand.

When there was a moment to relax, the crew members opened the mail they had picked up in Rockland.

For Arthur, there was a cassette from his little brother "to help him get to sleep." Listening to the tape through his headphones, he shook his head and laughed. "City sounds," he explained unplugging the headphones so C.T. could hear. "Home sweet home. What did you get?"

"Just some stamped envelopes addressed to my mother," the boy answered. "I don't know where she thought I'd mail them."

"Hey, Rachel. Did you get anything?" Arthur asked.

She shrugged. "Nothing special." Whatever "nothing special" was, Rachel didn't want to talk about it.

As the tracking continued, Ramon explained to C.T. how the automatic direction finder – or ADF – worked. "The arrow at the top of the ADF screen is the direction in which the bow of the *Mimi* is pointing. The red blip is the direction in which the ADF antenna is pointing. When the whale is on the surface, the antenna locks onto the radio tag's signal. The blip on the ADF screen shows us the location of the whale in re-lation to where we are. Then we can set a course to continue our tracking."

The whale had not surfaced for 19 minutes. C.T. was worried. "Maybe it drowned."

Ramon shook his head. "We think they can stay down for half an hour or longer if they have to."

Just then, the ADF began to beep. The whale was on the surface. C.T. recorded the whale's new location on his chart, and the Captain changed course to follow.

The crew members took turns monitoring the ADF. They tried to figure out what the whale's behavior meant.

"She seems to be staying in one place now," Arthur noted at one point.

"She's probably feeding," Sally Ruth suggested.

Before going to bed that night, Captain Granville listened to the weather report on the radio. Gusty winds and falling *air pressure* did not sound serious. But the Captain seemed worried.

Anne and Rachel had the late watch. They monitored the ADF and kept the *Mimi* on course. During the night, Anne found Rachel in the saloon staring at a crumpled envelope.

"Mail?" Anne asked quietly.

Rachel nodded. "I picked it up in Rockland. I should have left it there." She paused and then blurted out, "My parents are getting a divorce."

Rachel struggled to hold back tears. "It's always the same. All the bickering. They're a big, fat pain!"

Anne sat down next to her. "My parents finally got a divorce about two years ago," she said sympathetically. "I used to get tons of that kind of mail."

"Did the situation ever get any better?"

"Eventually," Anne answered. "You just have to hang in there."

Noticing the beep from the whale's radio tag, Anne asked, "How long has she been up?"

"About a minute," Rachel answered. "That's a long time between dives. Do you think the tag fell off?"

"I doubt it," Anne said. "She's probably just sleeping."

At last, Rachel was able to smile. "Something about a whale sleeping is funny." She and Anne laughed. "That reminds me," Rachel went on, "I could use some sleep myself."

Anne went back up on the deck. She was changing course based on the whale's new position, when Captain Granville came up.

"You had another hour's sleep coming," Anne said, surprised.

The Captain was uneasy. "Has it been this still all night?"

"We had some breeze earlier," Anne answered. "Is anything wrong?"

"Maybe just a feeling," the Captain replied, taking the wheel. "We'll see what the morning brings."

In the morning, the Captain checked the *barometer*. "Whale still moving east?" he asked Arthur.

"Northeast, last I heard," Arthur said. "She's been down a long time."

Captain Granville found Ramon and C.T. on deck. "I'm afraid we'll have to lose that whale of yours today," he said to Ramon. "I'd say we're in for a storm. The barometer hasn't fallen yet, but I don't like the looks of those clouds."

"What's a barometer?" C.T. asked.

"An instrument that measures the pressure of the *atmosphere*," Ramon explained. "When the atmospheric pressure falls, it usually means bad weather."

Just then, Arthur called to them from below. The radio tag's signal had not been picked up for more than 40 minutes. "I think we've lost her," Sally Ruth said sadly.

Rachel and Arthur scanned the horizon for the whale. The others watched the ADF. For what seemed like a long time, they waited in silence. Finally, the silence was broken by the sound of the whale's radio signal.

"That's great!" Anne exclaimed, and she checked the ADF screen for the whale's location. "Captain Granville, we've found our whale. We'd like to head east."

But Captain Granville had bad news. "We'll have to head for port," he told Anne. "We're in for a storm." And he pointed to the barometer.

At the Captain's cry of "All hands on deck!" the crew gathered around.

"The barometer just fell through the basement," Captain Granville announced. "We're in for a blow. With luck, we'll beat it back to Rockland. If not, we'll ride the storm out."

Then the Captain issued orders.

"Sally Ruth and C.T., go below and secure all loose gear. Arthur, break out the safety harnesses. I want everyone to wear one under his or her life jacket. All of you," he ordered, "get your foul weather gear and get moving."

The wind and the waves rose as the *Mimi* headed west toward Rockland. On all sides spray shot up and crashed over the deck. Dark clouds moved in from the eastern horizon. Could the *Mimi* beat the storm to Rockland?

Anne took the wheel. Already the boat was pitching and rolling like a live thing. The violent lurching finally took its toll in seasickness. Both C.T. and Rachel had to rush up on deck and hang

over the rail. The *Mimi* was being battered by wind-driven rain. Finally, the Captain turned to Anne.

"We'll never make it to Rockland! We'll have to get the sails down and run before the storm under bare poles."

Working against time and the weather, the crew began to take down the sails.

"Okay, let's get the *jib* down!" the Captain shouted. "Rachel, slack that halyard! Bring that *ring* in, Ramon!"

"It's stuck!" Ramon called.

The ring that held the jib stretched over the *bow* would not slide over the *bowsprit*. The Captain and Ramon pulled together. Still it would not budge.

"That block is fouled," the Captain said. "I'll have to go out there."

Then he climbed over the rail onto the *whisker stay*. With waves splashing over him, the Captain made his way slowly toward the bowsprit. Suddenly, a huge wave crashed against the boat. The whisker stay snapped, and Captain

Granville was swept into the swirling water!

"The Captain fell overboard!" Ramon shouted. "Get the ladder!"

Terrified, C.T. emerged from below and rushed to the rail just as his grandfather was pulled from the water.

"C.T., you get below and stay there!" Captain Granville ordered. "I'm all right."

Drenched and shivering, the Captain went straight back to work. He pointed to the jib flapping in the wind.

"With that whisker stay gone, the bowsprit could go any minute. We've got to get the rest of the sails down!"

"What happens if the bowsprit breaks?" Anne asked.

"We lose the *mast*," was the Captain's terse reply.

Below deck, C.T. and Rachel made a discovery. The *Mimi* was taking on water, and the cabin was awash. Captain Granville rushed below to check the cabin. C.T. saw him stagger.

"Grandpa, are you going to be all right?" C.T. asked.

"I'm going to be fine," the Captain answered, moving past C.T.

Then, above the roar of the storm, the crew heard a loud, wrenching CRACK!

"The bowsprit broke!" Ramon shouted above the din.

Back on deck, the Captain ordered Anne to start the *Mimi*'s engine. But when she turned the key, she got no response.

"It won't start!" she yelled to the Captain.

"There's land ahead!" he shouted to Anne. "If we're lucky, we can get through that break in the rocks and beach the boat!"

"But if we hit the rocks, we'll be smashed to splinters!" Anne shouted above the storm.

Below deck, Anne's terrifying words reached C.T. as all around him water rushed in flooding the *Mimi*. Could they survive this *storm*?

Playing Tag

The crew of the *Mimi* uses a special radio tag to gather data about a humpback whale. Using what they know about whales in general, plus the data from the radio tag, the members of the crew drew conclusions about the behavior of one whale.

The table below provides coded research data about what four subjects did during a 24-hour period. What does this information tell you about each subject?

First, use the map to see exactly where subjects were at different times. (For example, look across row 4 and down column D to find the cinema at 4D.) Then, based on the data you have and on what you know about human beings in general, draw some conclusions about the individual subjects.

1. Where does each subject spend the most time?
2. Which subject is probably *not* a human being? Why do you think so?
3. What clues are there to help you guess the age of each subject?
4. What might subjects be doing in the places indicated by question marks?

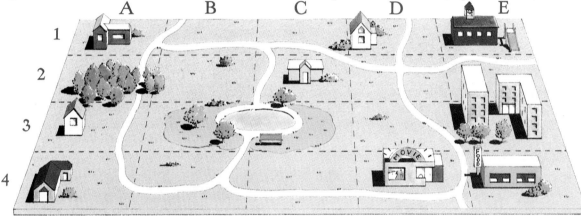

	TIME	BEHAVIOR	LOCATION
Subject 1	8:15–8:45 AM	Feeding	3-A
	10:00 AM–2:00 PM	Sleeping	3-A
	2:15–2:45 PM	Feeding	3-A
	4:00–4:45 PM	?	3-C
	4:45–5:00 PM	Sleeping	3-B
	5:10–6:00 PM	Sleeping	3-A
	6:15–7:00 PM	Feeding	3-A
	8:00 PM–3:00 AM	Sleeping	3-A
	3:15–3:45 AM	Feeding	3-A
	4:00–8:00 AM	Sleeping	3-A

	TIME	BEHAVIOR	LOCATION
Subject 2	8:00–8:20 AM	Feeding	4-A
	9:00 AM–12:45 PM	?	3-E
	1:00–2:00 PM	Feeding	4-E
	2:15–5:00 PM	?	3-E
	6:30–7:15 PM	Feeding	4-A
	8:30–10:45 PM	?	4-D
	11:30 PM–7:30 AM	Sleeping	4-A

	TIME	BEHAVIOR	LOCATION
Subject 3	8:00–8:12 AM	Feeding	2-C
	8:30 AM–12:20 PM	?	1-E
	12:30–1:00 PM	Feeding	1-E
	1:10–3:30 PM	?	1-E
	3:35–4:00 PM	Feeding	2-C
	4:05–5:15 PM	?	1-A, 3-C
	5:20–6:20 PM	?	2-C
	6:30–7:00 PM	Feeding	2-C
	7:15–8:15 PM	?	2-C
	9:00 PM–7:00 AM	Sleeping	2-C

	TIME	BEHAVIOR	LOCATION
Subject 4	7:55–7:58 AM	Feeding	2-C
	7:59–8:13 AM	Sleeping	2-C
	8:14–8:45 AM	?	2-A
	9:00 AM–1:30 PM	Sleeping	2-C
	2:00–4:30 PM	?	2-A, 3-A
		?	4-A, 3-A
		?	2-A, 1-A
	5:15–5:18 PM	Feeding	2-C
	5:20–8:00 PM	Sleeping	2-C
	8:15–8:30 PM	?	2-A, 3-A
	9:15 PM–12:05 AM	Sleeping	2-C
	12:06–12:10 AM	?	2-C
	12:11–3:00 AM	Sleeping	2-C
	3:01–3:07 AM	?	2-C
	3:08–7:15 AM	Sleeping	2-C
	7:20–7:54 AM	?	2-C, 2-A, 3-A

THE WORLD'S WORST WEATHER

Getting caught in a storm made the *Mimi's* crew members realize just how dangerous bad weather can be. Ben Affleck wondered where the worst weather in the world is. Some people say it's in New Hampshire on top of Mount Washington. At 6,288 feet, Mt. Washington is the highest peak in the northeastern United States, and part of a range of mountains called the Presidentials.

In late November, Ben visited the weather observatory at the top of Mt. Washington. Ken Rancourt, one of the meteorologists who studies the weather at the summit, met Ben at the base of the mountain. Ken is one of the six men who work at the Mt. Washington Observatory. In teams of three, the men work in shifts—one week on the job and one week off.

Ken and Ben traveled up the mountain's eight-mile road in a big machine that looked like a tractor, an army tank, and a snowplow combined. This is the only vehicle that can make it up the mountain in winter.

On the day of Ben's trip, it was raining at the bottom of the mountain and the road was hazardous. There was dense fog everywhere. Ben couldn't see much, and wasn't sure he wanted to. He knew that right near the road were sheer cliffs, dropping hundreds of feet. As the snow tractor climbed, the road conditions got worse. Halfway up the mountain, Ken radioed the Observatory to see how much worse conditions would get. The man at the top said that the temperature was 20 degrees and that the wind was averaging 60 miles an hour, with gusts up to 70. Ben thought they might have to turn back, but Ken kept going.

After a couple of hours, just when it was beginning to seem to Ben as if the trip would never end,

The highest wind speed ever recorded in the world occurred on Mt. Washington in 1934. A meteorologist clocked wind blasting at 231 miles per hour.

they finally reached the top. Everything was covered with ice. Looking outside the snow tractor at 11:30 A.M., it was hard to tell what time it was.

Ken and Ben climbed right from the snow tractor into the weather room. On the wall was a photograph of Mt. Washington, and Ben could finally see the route he had traveled and where he was now. The Observatory was founded in 1934, although the building now in use wasn't built until 1980. The Observatory does weather-related research, but its major function is a weather station. The staff studies the climate, and keeps track of the weather 24 hours a day.

Inside the weather station are dials and meters that give readings for temperature, wind speed, wind direction, and barometric pressure. But the instruments that actually take those readings are located outdoors. A lot of ice builds up on those instruments, and when it does, the readings are not accurate. So Ken and the other meteorologists have to go outside regularly and knock the ice off the instruments. At the same time, they collect a precipitation can to see how much rain or snow has fallen. At noon it was Ken's turn to go outside, and Ben volunteered to help him.

It was the first time on his trip that Ben had been outside without shelter. The temperature was 20 degrees Fahrenheit. The wind was blowing at 70 miles an hour, with gusts up to 90 miles per hour. Ben could hardly stand up and, like the instruments, his goggles got covered with ice. He could hardly see.

The wind was blowing at 70 miles per hour when Ken and Ben went out to knock ice off the instruments.

Ken helped Ben change the precipitation can. The average annual snowfall on the mountain is 250 inches, or over 20 feet. But this time, the can was nearly empty. There hadn't been much rain or snow. Why then, Ben wondered, was there ice all over everything? Ken explained that the ice, called rime ice, is actually frozen cloud. The little droplets of moisture that make up a cloud freeze when they hit the instruments, and the ice slowly builds up in beautiful long "feathers." Looking at the ice feathers, Ben could tell the direction which the wind was blowing in. He thought the rime ice looked like furry icicles, pointing sideways.

At 1:00 P.M., back inside, it was time for Ken to send the weather report to the National Weather Service. Someone has to call in the mountain conditions every three hours, 24 hours a day. Ken let Ben do it. Here's what Ben reported:

> temperature - 22 degrees Fahrenheit
> wind - 80 miles an hour,
> with gusts up to 104
> barometer - 29 inches
> visibility - zero
> icing - moderate

By 6:00 P.M. the weather instruments were misreading again, which meant that the rime ice had built up. It was dark out. Ben was hungry and the wind was now blowing at 100 miles an hour. But he was there to help as well as to learn, so Ben bundled up again and went back outside with Ken. He and Ken used crowbars to steady themselves but, even so, they kept falling down. When they were finished, Ken told Ben he'd done a good day's work, and had certainly earned his dinner.

At the dinner table, Ben asked the scientists why Mt. Washington has the world's worst weather. After all, there are hundreds of higher mountain peaks, and many of them are in colder climates. Ken and the others explained.

The Presidential Mountains run from north to south and the land around them is low. When air moves out of the west toward Mt. Washington, it has to climb 4,000 feet to the top. At the top it runs into the atmospheric layer called the *tropopause*, which acts as a lid on the moving air. Now, as this wind squeezes between the top of Mt. Washington and the tropopause, it speeds up. So, a 10-mile-an-hour wind at the base of the mountain may become an 80-mile-an-hour wind as it climbs over the top.

Mt. Washington is cold, too. The highest temperature ever recorded there is only 72 degrees Fahrenheit. The lowest is 47 degrees below zero, and the average is 27 degrees, the lowest average temperature in the United States outside Alaska.

But high winds and low temperatures are not the whole story. Mt. Washington lies in the center of three major storm tracks. These storm centers come up the east coast, up the Mississippi and Ohio River Valleys, and along the Great Lakes and the St. Lawrence River. And where do they meet? At Mt. Washington, of course! There may be some mountain peaks in the Arctic or Antarctic that have worse weather, but no one is there to measure it.

Ben delivered the Mt. Washington weather report to the National Weather Service.

The next morning, Ben witnessed the most breathtaking, crystal-clear dawn of his life. The clouds were breaking up on the summit, and the view stretched for miles. On the horizon he could see the sun's reflection on a narrow strip of orange. Ken said that was the Atlantic Ocean, 85 miles away. Ben finally got a look at the other buildings on the summit. There were giant microwave antennas for transmitting local television signals. There was the original observatory, now closed. And there was also an old building that used to be a hotel. Ben wondered who would take a vacation up on top of Mt. Washington.

On the way down the mountain, Ben got to see all the scary, exciting, and beautiful sights he'd missed on the way up. The sun made everything stand out brightly. As the snow tractor got near the bottom of Mt. Washington, Ben felt like he was returning from another planet. And in a way, he was. He had just visited a whole new world of weather. Some people call it the world's worst. But on that crystal morning, Ben thought it just might be the world's best.

The clouds were breaking up on the summit, and the view stretched for miles. Ben could see a narrow strip of orange shining on the horizon. Ken said that it was the sun's reflection on the Atlantic Ocean, 85 miles away.

Now that you know the reasons for the weather on Mt. Washington, see if you can figure out the reasons for the weather where you live. For one month, keep a record of daily rainfall and high and low temperatures for your town. (You can get this information from the newspaper.) Use a map of your own region to study the land forms and bodies of water surrounding the region. As you gather information, think about these questions and then raise questions of your own: Is your region generally hot or cold? wet or dry? Is its altitude high or low? Is it near mountains or bodies of water? Does it have any conditions similar to those on Mt. Washington?

SHIPWRECKED

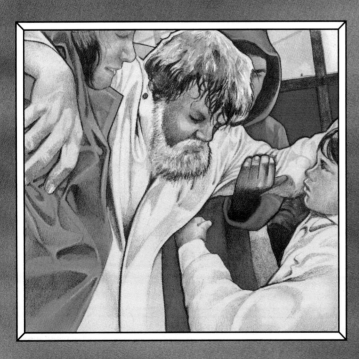

When the raging storm subsided, the crippled *Mimi* was aground in a partly sheltered cove. Ramon had hurt his hand. The others were exhausted but seemed to be okay. They set to work. Rain fell steadily as they loaded food, equipment, and gear into the dory for the short trip to shore.

The Captain stood in the shallow water, directing the work. "C.T., get into the boat," he said weakly.

"Captain Granville, are you all right?" Anne asked.

"Into . . . the . . . boat, C.T.," the Captain said again, leaning on the dory for support.

Then, as he struggled to haul the loaded dory to shore, the Captain collapsed in the water.

"Captain Granville!" Anne shouted, rushing to him. The others followed.

Quickly, the group lifted the unconscious man and carried him to the shore.

"What happened?" asked Arthur.

"He got too cold," Anne answered.

"*Hypothermia*?" Rachel asked.

Anne nodded. "Looks like it," she said gravely.

In the rain they worked quickly to remove the Captain's wet clothes and cover him.

"Will he be all right?" C.T. asked.

Anne reassured him. "C.T., we'll take care of him. You and Sally Ruth go back to the *Mimi*. Get the storm jib and more blankets."

"Bring the ax, too," added Ramon, "and some extra line."

"How does it look?" Ramon asked quietly.

Anne shook her head.

Soon Rachel and Sally Ruth were putting up a makeshift shelter using logs, rope, and one of the *Mimi*'s sails.

C.T. was frightened. He didn't understand what had happened to his grandfather.

"Your grandfather has hypothermia, C.T.," Ramon explained. "That means his body temperature has dropped too low. We have to find a way to raise his temperature."

C.T. bent over the Captain. "Grandpa? Grandpa? . . ." he whispered. The old sailor lay motionless, his eyes closed.

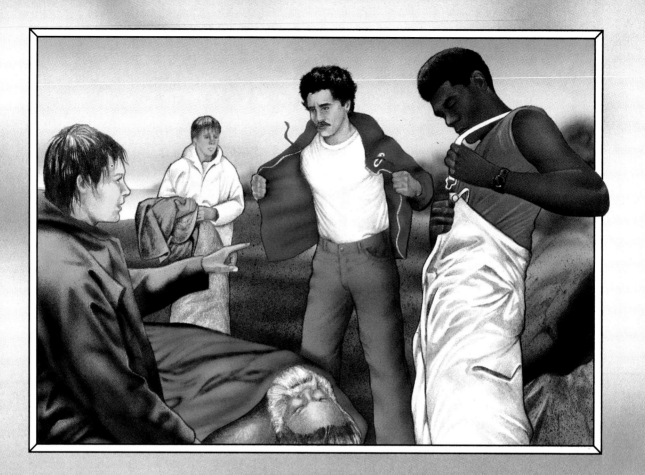

"How can we warm him up?" said Arthur, his voice strained.

"There's only one way – body heat," Anne answered. "Somebody's got to lie next to him under the blankets."

Immediately C.T. volunteered. But Anne chose Ramon and Arthur because they were bigger. Quickly, they took off their wet clothes and crawled under the blankets on each side of the unconscious Captain.

"We've got to sandwich him between us," Ramon explained to Arthur, "to bring his body temperature up."

"Man, he's **cold!**" said Arthur.

Anne agreed. "Let's just hope he doesn't get **too** cold."

"What if he does?" Arthur asked.

Anne and Ramon glanced at each other. Their worried faces answered Arthur's question. They would have to wait and see if the flow of heat from Ramon's and Arthur's bodies could save the Captain.

Eager to help, C.T. offered to build a fire. With Sally Ruth and Rachel, he went off to gather wood.

"Get the branches at the bottom of the trees. That's where they'll be drier," C.T. instructed.

Sally Ruth added, "And get small stuff for kindling to start the fire."

C.T. may have been inexperienced at sea, but on land he knew what he was doing. Before long, he had built a fine blazing fire. "Birch bark burns even when it's wet," he pointed out.

While everyone waited to see if the Captain would recover, Anne bandaged Ramon's injured hand.

"That's a bad rope burn," Anne said as she covered the wound with gauze.

"I held onto Captain Granville's lifeline when he fell overboard," Ramon explained.

Just then . . .

"Hey! The Captain moved!" shouted Arthur.

C.T. came running. "Grandpa? Grandpa!" he cried.

Captain Granville stirred feebly. "C.T.?" he murmured, opening his eyes.

"Everybody okay?" he asked. "And the boat?" C.T. nodded and smiled, feeling relieved.

"We're all fine," Anne said. "How do **you** feel?"

The Captain nodded—a sign that he was recovering. Then he fell off to sleep.

With Captain Granville out of danger, the castaways were free to deal with other problems. The tide had gone out, and the *Mimi* was sitting in mud.

Examining the ship's exposed hull, Rachel made a disturbing discovery. "Uh-oh," she said. "The storm opened up a seam."

"That's where the water got in," Arthur confirmed.

Rachel looked out toward the water. "If we don't get it fixed fast," she said matter-of-factly, "when the tide rises, this boat won't rise with it. Let's go to work," she continued. "I think I can caulk it. My father taught me how."

While Rachel and Sally Ruth started the repair work on the *Mimi*'s hull, Arthur tried out the radio. "MAYDAY, MAYDAY. This is the *Mimi* calling. MAYDAY." No response. "This thing is shot," Arthur muttered, as he carried the radio ashore.

Meanwhile, Anne and Ramon discussed the next order of business—finding out just where they were. "I'll scout the area," Ramon volunteered.

"Good idea," said Anne. "There's probably a town on the other side of these woods." Grinning, she added, "We can call a taxi."

Ramon smiled. "I'll take C.T. with me. Maybe we can find a house or something."

As the explorers started off, Ramon consulted his compass. "On the way back, we'll set a course due east – 180 degrees in the opposite direction to the one we're going in now," he explained to C.T. "That'll put us right back in camp."

C.T., however, was using another method to help them find their way back.

"What are you doing?"

"Blazing a trail," answered C.T.

From time to time C.T. broke twigs on a tree or bush.

Ramon was embarrassed that he hadn't thought of this simple but reliable method. "Good idea," he said sheepishly. "Uh ... kind of backup for the compass."

As they made their way through the woods, C.T. and Ramon talked about what had happened to Captain Granville.

"A lot of people swim in the ocean in the summer," C.T. pointed out, "and they don't get hypothermia."

"Yes," Ramon agreed, "but after your grandfather fell overboard, he never got dry. His clothes were soaked and the wind made him even colder. He was exhausted, but he had to keep working to get us to shore. His body just couldn't take it and he went into shock. His heartbeat slowed way down, and finally he passed out."

"Could he have died?" C.T. asked.

Ramon nodded yes. "His temperature dropped to eighty-five or ninety degrees. If it had gone much lower, he could have died."

C.T. walked on in silence, thinking about what Ramon had just said.

The scouts went on for a while without finding any signs of other people. Finally, they decided to survey the area from a treetop. Ramon couldn't go

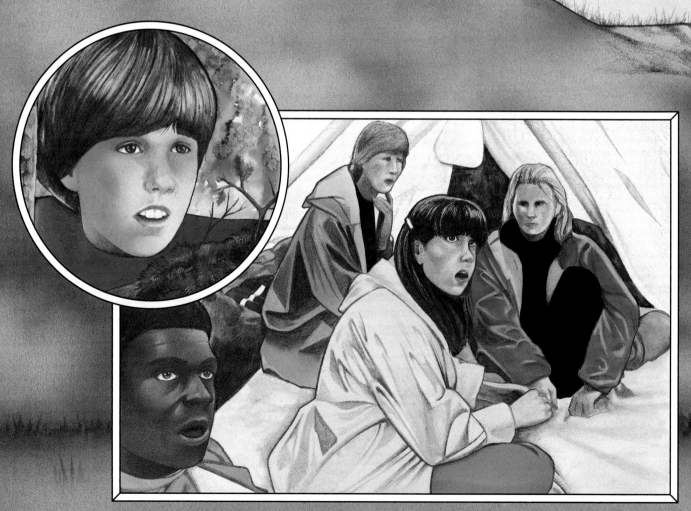

up because of his injured hand. So C.T. made the hard and dangerous climb to the top of a tall evergreen.

Near the top of the tree, C.T. had a clear view in all directions. "Uh-oh," he muttered, looking north, south, east, and west. What he saw really worried him.

"We're on an island," C.T. announced, when he and Ramon returned to the camp.

The others were astonished. "No roads? No houses? No people?" Anne asked.

"Nothing," Ramon confirmed. "C.T. couldn't even see the mainland."

On an island! What would they do now? Their boat was damaged, their radio was broken, their food supply was limited, the Captain was sick . . . .

Anne was quick to answer the look of concern on each face: "We'll take things one at a time, okay? Just as we've been doing. We've got food and shelter.

The Captain's out of danger." She turned to Arthur. "Can you fix the radio?"

Arthur shrugged. "I don't know . . . I can try. I may have to use some parts from Erik's whale tag receiver."

Suddenly, the whale tag receiver began to beep.

"Hey, it's working!" Arthur shouted. "It's picking up the signal from our whale!"

Everyone in the shelter turned to look at the blinking lights of the receiver. C.T. turned toward the gray ocean.

"Wow," he said quietly. "You mean our whale's out there, right near us?"

"Yeah," Rachel sighed. "But where's that? We don't even know where we are."

The great sea rolled on and the fog closed in, cutting them off from the rest of the world. The crew of the *Mimi* felt very much alone.

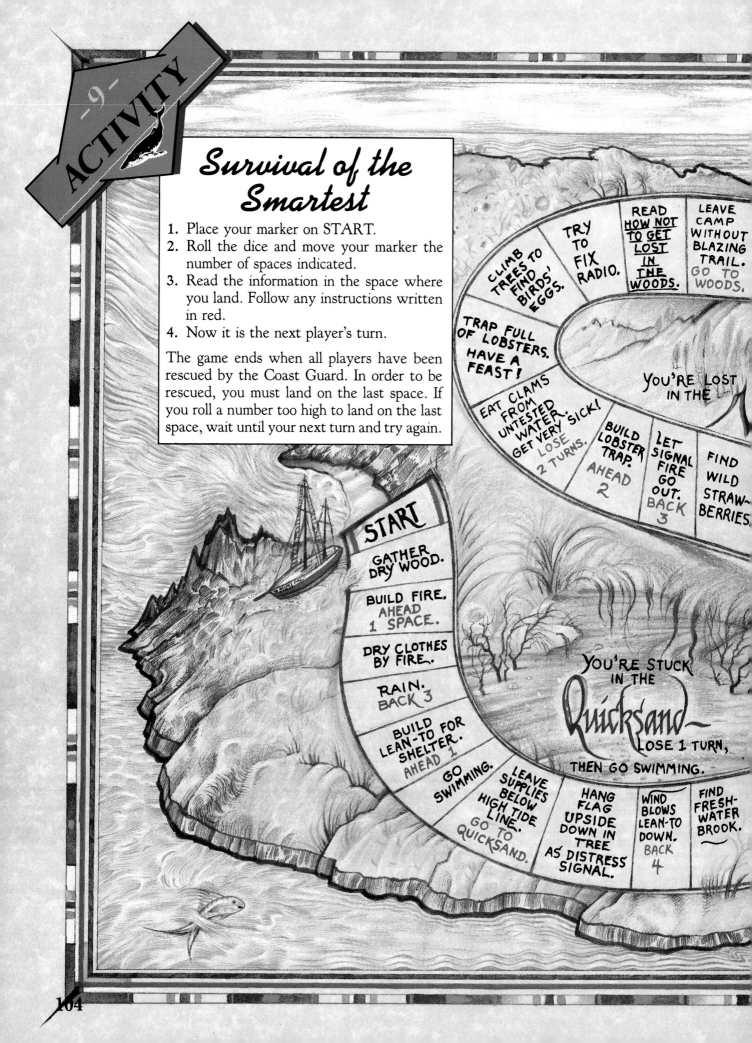

Survival of the Smartest

1. Place your marker on START.
2. Roll the dice and move your marker the number of spaces indicated.
3. Read the information in the space where you land. Follow any instructions written in red.
4. Now it is the next player's turn.

The game ends when all players have been rescued by the Coast Guard. In order to be rescued, you must land on the last space. If you roll a number too high to land on the last space, wait until your next turn and try again.

CLIMB TREES TO FIND BIRDS' EGGS.

TRY TO FIX RADIO.

READ HOW NOT TO GET LOST IN THE WOODS.

LEAVE CAMP WITHOUT BLAZING TRAIL. GO TO WOODS.

TRAP FULL OF LOBSTERS. HAVE A FEAST!

YOU'RE LOST IN THE

EAT CLAMS FROM UNTESTED WATER. GET VERY SICK! LOSE 2 TURNS.

BUILD LOBSTER TRAP. AHEAD 2

LET SIGNAL FIRE GO OUT. BACK 3

FIND WILD STRAW-BERRIES.

START

GATHER DRY WOOD.

BUILD FIRE, AHEAD 1 SPACE.

DRY CLOTHES BY FIRE.

RAIN. BACK 3

BUILD LEAN-TO FOR SHELTER. AHEAD 1

GO SWIMMING.

LEAVE SUPPLIES BELOW HIGH TIDE LINE. GO TO QUICKSAND.

YOU'RE STUCK IN THE Quicksand— LOSE 1 TURN, THEN GO SWIMMING.

HANG FLAG UPSIDE DOWN IN TREE AS DISTRESS SIGNAL.

WIND BLOWS LEAN-TO DOWN. BACK 4

FIND FRESH-WATER BROOK.

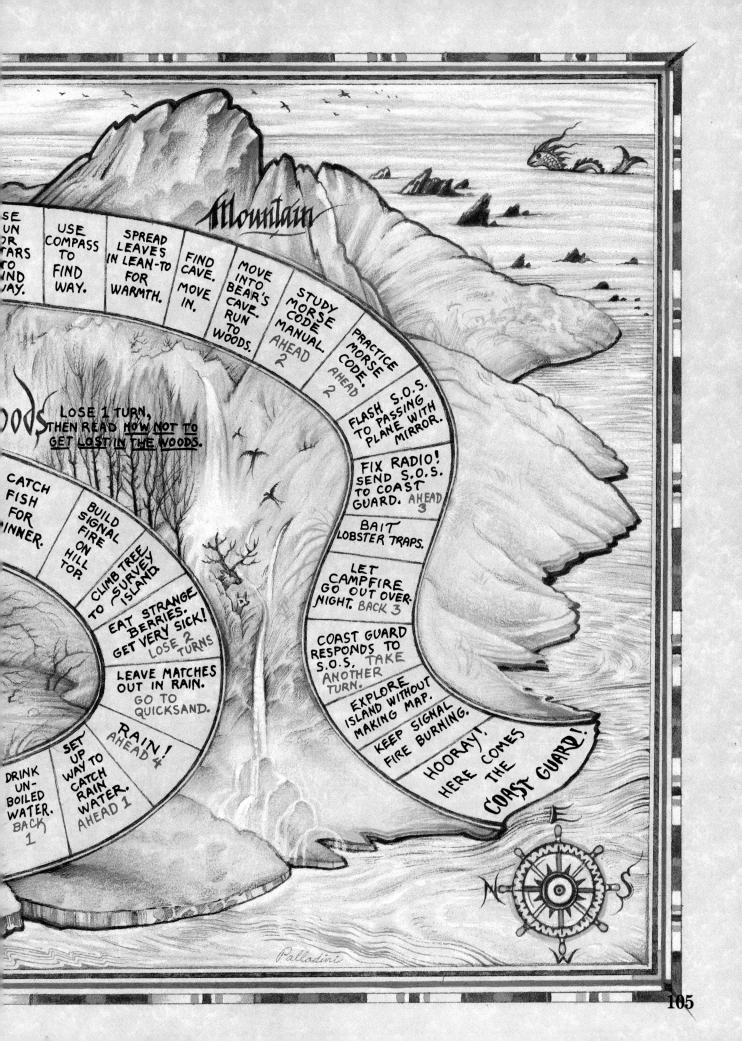

SE UN OR TARS TO IND AY.

USE COMPASS TO FIND WAY.

SPREAD LEAVES IN LEAN-TO FOR WARMTH.

FIND CAVE. MOVE IN.

MOVE INTO BEAR'S CAVE. RUN TO WOODS.

STUDY MORSE CODE MANUAL. AHEAD 2

PRACTICE MORSE CODE. AHEAD 2

Mountain

ods

LOSE 1 TURN, THEN READ HOW NOT TO GET LOST IN THE WOODS.

FLASH S.O.S. TO PASSING PLANE WITH MIRROR.

FIX RADIO! SEND S.O.S. TO COAST GUARD. AHEAD 3

BAIT LOBSTER TRAPS.

CATCH FISH FOR INNER.

BUILD SIGNAL FIRE ON HILL TOP.

CLIMB TREE TO SURVEY ISLAND.

EAT STRANGE BERRIES. GET VERY SICK! LOSE 2 TURNS

LEAVE MATCHES OUT IN RAIN. GO TO QUICKSAND.

LET CAMPFIRE GO OUT OVER-NIGHT. BACK 3

COAST GUARD RESPONDS TO S.O.S. TAKE ANOTHER TURN.

EXPLORE ISLAND WITHOUT MAKING MAP.

KEEP SIGNAL FIRE BURNING.

DRINK UN-BOILED WATER. BACK 1

SET UP WAY TO CATCH RAIN WATER. AHEAD 1

RAIN! AHEAD 4

HOORAY! HERE COMES THE COAST GUARD!

Palladini

N
S
E
W

GOOSE BUMPS

In "The Voyage of the *Mimi*" it didn't take Captain Granville very long to get hypo-thermia when he fell into the Gulf of Maine. It was a surprise to the cast and crew working on the film that someone could get hypothermia so fast, even in summer. Ben Affleck, who plays C.T., wanted to learn more about hypo-thermia and about how the body controls its tem-perature. So he went to visit Dr. Murray Hamlet at the United States Army Research Institute of Envi-ronmental Medicine in Natick, Massachusetts. Here scientists study how the body reacts to ex-treme heat and cold. Dr. Hamlet is the chief of the Cold Division.

Like many people, Ben assumed that our bodies have a temperature of 98.6 degrees Fahrenheit all over. But Dr. Hamlet explained that only our *core* temperature is 98.6 degrees. The body's core is the torso, where the heart and other organs are located. This area is crucial for survival, and the body works to maintain a steady core temperature.

The heat in our bodies is created when we digest food. In digestion, food is broken down into glucose — sugar — which goes to organs and muscles along with oxygen. Our organs and muscles use the glucose and oxygen in a chemical burning process that creates heat. Blood carries the heat through arteries and veins to all parts of the body.

Sometimes our bodies get too hot. When this happens, our brain gets a message that the core is becoming uncomfortably warm. Our brain then sends a message to our *extremities* — our arms and legs — that some heat needs to be released. The blood vessels in the skin on our extremities then release some of the heat that is traveling in our blood. Heat radiates off the skin and cooled blood flows back to the core.

If we are outside in very cold weather, the same process occurs in reverse. The body tells the brain that it is cold. The brain sends a message back through the body to shut off the blood vessels close to the skin in the extremities. Then the blood stays closer to the core and is not exposed to the cooling effects of the environment.

Dr. Hamlet wanted Ben to get a clear idea of how the body controls heat. He attached three *ther-mistors* to Ben. A thermistor is a temperature-measuring device for the outside of the body. He at-tached one to Ben's chest, one to his arm, and one to his fingertip. Right away Ben could see that there was a big difference in temperatures. The thermistor on his chest indicated the warmest temperature, which was only 92 degrees. (It wasn't 98.6 degrees because it was outside of his core, on his skin.) The one on his arm read 89 degrees, and the one on his fingertip read only 88 degrees. Ben was surprised that the temperature of his extremities could be so low and he could still feel comfortable.

But Ben was in for some big surprises. Dr. Hamlet was preparing the Arctic Chamber to show Ben how his body temperatures would change when he was exposed to cold. The Arctic Chamber can get as cold as 70 degrees below zero. When Ben and Dr. Hamlet entered the Chamber, the temperature was 30 degrees and dropping.

After a few minutes, they checked the readings on Ben's thermistors. The one on his chest read 90 degrees. The one on his arm read 75 degrees. And the temperature on his fingertip had fallen all the way to 63 degrees! Ben felt very cold. The temperatures in his extremities were decreasing while his body maintained its core temperature. Proof of this was that a thermometer in Ben's mouth still read about 98 degrees.

Dr. Hamlet explained some of Ben's other reactions to the cold. For instance, the goose bumps all over his arms were a reaction left over from ancient times when our ancestors, like apes, were covered with hair. Then, the purpose of goose bumps was to raise the hair on their bodies, so that the hair could trap more warm air. Dr. Hamlet said that Ben's shivering was a form of involuntary exercise. It is something our muscles do automatically to try to keep warm. But shivering wasn't going to help Ben because the air around him was too cold. He needed *insulation*, something to hold in heat. Dr. Hamlet gave Ben a big parka to wear. Now the heat that his body was producing would be trapped by the jacket and Ben would feel warmer.

The temperature in the Arctic Chamber was now a little less than 20 degrees. Ben was ready for warmer temperatures, but there was one more cold experiment to do. Dr. Hamlet wanted to demonstrate the effect of wind chill. The Arctic Chamber has a gigantic fan that can create wind at different speeds. Dr. Hamlet ordered a 10-mile-an-hour wind, and Ben could hear it coming. Suddenly he felt much colder.

The instrument behind Ben in this picture is called an anemometer, *and it measures wind speed. Ben couldn't believe how cold that wind made him feel when he was in the Arctic Chamber.*

"The room temperature is the same," said Dr. Hamlet, "but the warm air layer that has been surrounding your body is being blown away. Now you have to produce more heat to keep yourself warm. Let's take your hat off. Feel how much faster your face cools?" Ben could only nod his head. "Put your fingers out in the breeze. See how fast they cool?" Ben looked at the reading for the thermistor on his fingertip. Forty-five degrees! "Am I going to get frostbite?" he asked.

Before that could happen, they left the Arctic Chamber. Dr. Hamlet told Ben that, as bad as the cold air had been, cold water would have been much worse. "Water cools the body twenty-six times faster than air does," he said. "That's why people who fall into water get hypothermia. They lose so much heat to the water that they can't replace it, no matter how hard they shiver or swim."

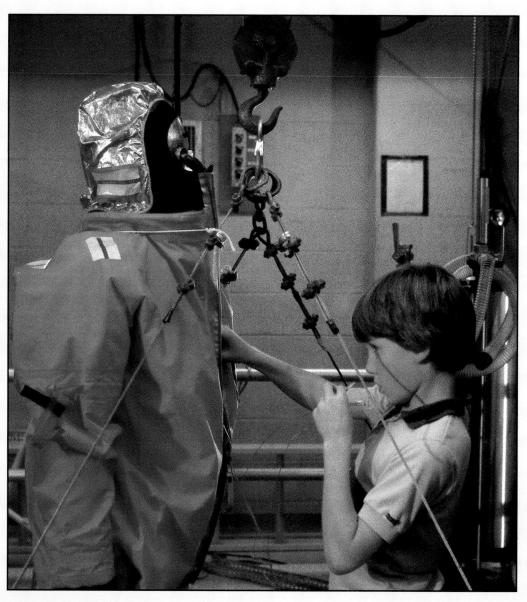

This time, Captain Nemo was the guinea pig instead of Ben. He was covered with the thermistors just like the ones Ben wore.

To prove this point, Dr. Hamlet took Ben to another lab and introduced him to Dr. Richard Gonzalez, a thermophysicist. Dr. Gonzalez works with a copper dummy called Captain Nemo. Captain Nemo has electrical coils inside his body which imitate the way that a human body creates, spreads, and conserves heat. The dummy is made of copper because this metal is an excellent conductor of heat. Captain Nemo is covered with thermistors.

Captain Nemo was being used to test a lightweight, waterproof survival suit in water that was 68 degrees. That may not sound very cold, but it is the average water temperature in places where boating accidents often occur.

The first time Captain Nemo was dunked in the pool he was wearing his survival suit. The second time he was dunked, he wasn't wearing it. Both times the thermistors were connected to a computer which gave a constant readout of his body temperature.

With the survival suit, Captain Nemo's "skin" temperature dropped only to 89 degrees. Without the suit, Captain Nemo's surface temperature became the same temperature as the water, 68 degrees, in just 10 minutes. Even if he had been wearing regular clothes, the results would have been nearly the same. Regular clothes get wet and then can't protect the skin from water so the body loses heat. Ben was beginning to understand how Captain Granville could get hypothermia from his quick dunk in the Gulf of Maine.

Toward the end of the day, Ben joined Dr. Hamlet beside a pond. Lots of Canadian geese were swimming around, and the 40-degree water didn't seem to bother them at all. Dr. Hamlet explained that this is because their feathers, which are coated with oil, provide insulation. Water never touches the skin under their feathers, only the skin on their feet. But here again they are well protected: in their legs they have valves that shut off the blood flow to

Captain Nemo's temperature falls to dangerous levels when he is lowered into cold water without his survival suit. But geese can live in cold water because their oil-coated feathers insulate their bodies.

their feet. If blood were to travel through their feet, the water would cool it to dangerously low temperatures. As the blood flowed back to their bodies, the geese would become hypothermic.

Ben mentioned that some whales live in Arctic waters where it is extremely cold. He wondered how they survived. Dr. Hamlet described the tremendous thickness of blubber, or fat, covering whales' bodies. This blubber is an excellent insulator. Plus, the whale is a very large animal. A large *mass* with a small surface area, like a whale, cools more slowly than a small mass and a large surface area. We humans have a lot of surface area but our mass is not so large. Because of their round bodies and thick blubber, whales can keep normal body temperatures, even in freezing water.

By the time Ben left the Army research lab, his body had been through a lot. But he had learned about *thermoregulation*—one of his body's most important processes.

Find out about the effect of wind on temperature. Try this:

1. Dip your hand in a bowl of water and let it dry in the breeze of an electric fan. (Do not put your fingers close to the fan!) Is your cool feeling a result of a drop in air temperature because of the breeze? Find out:

2. You'll need two thermometers and a friend. The thermometers should both show the same temperature when you start the experiment. Hold one thermometer directly in the breeze of the fan. Have your friend hold the other one near the fan, but not in the breeze. Does the thermometer in the breeze show a cooler temperature? How do you explain the difference between what your wet hand in the breeze felt and what the thermometer in the breeze measures?

109

MAKING DEW

The morning after the shipwreck, C.T. was up early. Armed with navigation charts from the *Mimi*, he climbed atop some rocks above the shore. There he tried to figure out where he and the other castaways were.

When he returned to the shelter, the others were just beginning to stir.

"How are you feeling, Grandpa?" he asked.

"Better, thanks," the Captain replied.

Rachel yawned. "I dreamed about the whale we tagged," she muttered.

"I guess she's gone now," Arthur said sleepily.

"Smart whale," Rachel answered. "I wish I were gone from this place."

"Guess we better try to figure out where we are," the Captain announced.

"That won't be easy," said Ramon. "The navigation equipment is pretty well shot."

"Where's that large-scale chart?" the Captain asked, rummaging through the gear.

"Here," C.T. said, holding up the chart. "I think we're on Seal Island. This

is the cove where we beached the *Mimi*." And he pointed to a spot he had circled on the large-scale chart.

To check their position, Captain Granville and C.T. took all the charts down to the rocks. C.T. pointed out the islands he had used as landmarks to pinpoint their location.

"This is Seal Island, all right," the Captain agreed. "Good work, son."

Back at the shelter, Captain Granville explained the situation. "We're well out of the main shipping lanes. There aren't likely to be many ships coming by here to see us or pick us up. Looks like we'll have to get ourselves out of here." The Captain looked around at his crew. "First thing, we've got to plug that leak in the *Mimi*."

"We did that already," Rachel said.

"Then we've got to pump her out," the Captain went on.

"We did that too," said Rachel.

"She floats at high tide," Sally Ruth added.

"But every time the tide goes out, she's back on her side. She ought to be moved to deeper water," Rachel concluded.

"You mean you haven't done that too?" he asked. There was a twinkle in Captain Granville's eye.

Aboard the *Mimi*, Captain Granville and Rachel surveyed the damage.

"That was one bad storm," Rachel said, looking at the tangled rigging and broken bowsprit. "Can we fix this mess?"

"We'll have to," the Captain answered. "We'll never be able to maneuver this vessel without a jib. And in order to use the jib, we need a bowsprit. That means we have to make a new one."

"There's no way to use the engine?" Rachel wondered.

The Captain shook his head. "Not with the starter soaked with sea water."

The crew members pitched in to remove the broken bowsprit and float it to shore. Then they raised the staysail and the mizzen and took the *Mimi* out of the cove and anchored her in deeper water.

Back on shore they opened the plastic containers of fresh water they had taken from the boat's tanks. Arthur took a drink. "Ughh!" he said, spitting the water out. "It's salty!"

"Sea water must have gotten into the tanks during the storm," the Captain concluded after checking the water. "This is too salty to drink. We'd better find some water on this island. We can't count on another rainstorm right away."

The castaways split up into teams and scoured the island for water. When they returned to the campsite, all reported the same dismal news. There was no fresh water anywhere.

"How long can somebody last without water?" Arthur asked.

Ramon shrugged. "It varies. A week . . . maybe more, maybe less."

Suddenly, Captain Granville shouted at C.T. "What are you doing?"

C.T. had dipped his hand into the water in the cove and was raising it to his mouth.

"I'm getting a drink," he said. "I thought I could get used to the taste."

"It doesn't have anything to do with taste," his grandfather said vehemently. "Don't any of you drink sea water. Salt will dry you out. You'll get *dehydrated,* and you'll die."

Rachel frowned. "Yeah, but if it doesn't rain . . ."

Immediately Sally Ruth thought of a possible solution to the problem. "If we could build a still," she said, "we could use all this sea water."

"What's a still?" C.T. asked.

"It's a device you use to purify water," Sally Ruth replied.

Anne explained. "You heat the water to turn it into *vapor,* and the salt gets left behind. Then you cool the vapor until it turns back into water."

As the group was pondering the idea, Rachel made a discovery. "Hey, you guys! Look!" She pointed to the plastic sheet draped over a pile of gear. The inside of the plastic was covered with tiny drops of water. The others gathered around.

"Where did the water come from?" C.T. asked. "Is it dew?"

"It's like dew," Anne said. "It's called condensation."

Rachel touched the inside of the plastic sheet. Drops of water were running down the sheet.

"That's it!" Sally Ruth exclaimed. "We can use the sun to heat the water!"

"A *solar still!*" cried Ramon.

Under the guidance of Sally Ruth and Ramon, the group began to build a solar still. First, they cleared an area and dug a triangle-shaped pit in the sand. They banked the outside of the pit to create sloping walls on the sides. With some clear plastic sheeting taken from the *Mimi*, they lined the pit and covered the ground around it. They placed a black plastic garbage bag on top of the clear plastic in the pit.

"The dark plastic of the garbage bag will absorb the heat," Ramon explained. "That will make the evaporation happen faster."

114

Next, they strung thin wire very tightly between stakes driven into the ground. The wire ran over the plastic sheeting along the sloping outside walls on two sides of the pit. Rocks were placed in the pit to hold the plastic in place. Then the pit was filled with sea water.

Using tree limbs, they rigged a frame over the pit and pulled the clear plastic sheeting up over it, taping it firmly in place. Now, the pit was completely enclosed in the plastic tent. The wire along the sides of the pit held the plastic against the sloping walls, creating a funnel. The lowest end of the funnel extended over a shallow bowl.

Sally Ruth explained how the still would work. "The energy of the sunlight goes through the clear plastic tent and heats up the water in the pit. The warm water turns into vapor — that's called *evaporation*. The vapor rises, leaving the salt behind."

"When the water vapor rises and hits the plastic tent," Ramon continued, "it cools enough to turn back into liquid — that's called *condensation*. The drops collect on the plastic, run down the sides, and are funneled down to the end and into the collecting bowl."

"The still will take a long time to make only a little fresh water," Anne pointed out. "We'll still have to ration water carefully."

"There's more plastic sheeting on the *Mimi*," the Captain said. "How about rigging up a couple more of these outfits?"

Before long, three solar stills glistened in the afternoon sun which beat down steadily. The thirsty crew of the *Mimi* waited and hoped that the makeshift stills would work. And they did work! The sea water evaporated. Vapor rose to the plastic and cooled. Fresh water collected in drops and ran down the sides of the stills. Slowly, slowly, water dripped into the bowls.

The first drink went to Sally Ruth for coming up with the idea for the still. Then the others took their turns.

The castaways had solved a life-threatening problem. Their solar stills were turning sea water into drinking water.

Arthur, meanwhile, was tinkering with the radio. Suddenly, it picked up a transmission and the crew heard the faint voice of the Coast Guard:

"Vessel name, *Mimi*. Vessel name, *Mimi*. Massachusetts registry. Unaccounted for and believed missing. Owner, Granville, Clement Tyler. Persons in crew . . ."

The voice trailed off into static. C.T. turned to his grandfather. "Then they're searching for us?"

"Possibly," the Captain replied. "Arthur, can you transmit with that radio?"

Arthur shook his head. "Not yet. It's only half fixed—the listening half."

The brief moment of excitement turned into gloom.

"They said 'believed' missing," C.T. said.

"Man, they better believe it," Arthur sighed.

"My parents must think I've drowned," Rachel mused. "All our families must think we've died at sea."

The stranded crew stared out at the shimmering, empty sea.

"The only people who know we're okay is us," C.T. said quietly.

"And we can't tell anybody," Arthur added.

Water, Water Everywhere... and Not a Drop to Drink

The *Mimi*'s crew is left high and dry without a fresh water supply . . . until they build a solar still.

You can observe the processes of evaporation and condensation by building your own solar still.

You Will Need

paper cup, pencil, string (two 40 cm lengths, one 25 cm length), clear plastic bag, salt

Steps

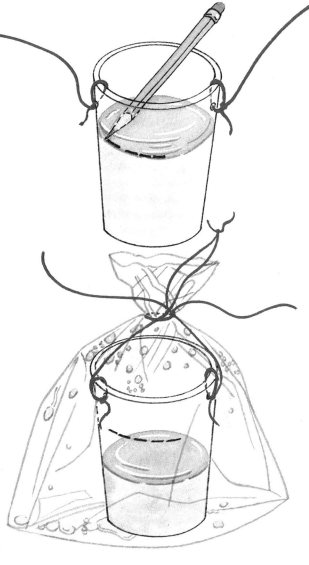

- Punch holes with a pencil in opposite sides of the paper cup, near the rim.
- Put one end of each 40 cm string through a hole and make knots to hold the strings in place.
- Fill the cup half-full with water. Use a pencil to mark the water line on the inside of the cup.
- Add 1 teaspoon of salt to the water. Mix well.
- Tie the strings in a knot about 25 cm from their ends. Tie another knot at their ends.
- Hang the cup in the sunniest spot you can find, indoors or out.
- Pull the plastic bag up over the cup. With the short string, tie the bag closed above the lower knot.
- Wait until water begins to condense inside the bag. Be patient! A solar still cannot work on rainy or cloudy days. It may take a few days, even in sunny weather.

Observations

- Why does the water evaporate?
- Why does water condense inside the bag?
- What is the source of the condensation?
- Examine the water that collects in the bottom of the bag. What does it look like? What does it taste like?

WATER, WATER EVERYWHERE

Stranded on the island without fresh water, the *Mimi*'s crew had an interesting problem. Although they were surrounded by water, they couldn't drink any of it. At least one town in the United States has the same problem. Greenport, New York, on the tip of Long Island, is surrounded by sea water. But the town's drinking water comes from an underground reservoir called an *aquifer*. Certain chemical pesticides, sprayed on local potato fields for a number of years, have accumulated in the aquifer. Because of the pollution threat, wells are being closed down by the Health Department. Where can the people of Greenport go for water? One possible solution is the ocean. Dr. Ted Taylor, a *physicist* and founder of a company called Nova, Inc., has been hired to help Greenport make drinking water from sea water. Ben Affleck visited Ted in Greenport one winter day.

Ted Taylor started his career as a nuclear physicist. In 1949 he went to work on nuclear bombs at the Los Alamos National Laboratory. For six years he worked on the design of bombs, trying to make them lighter, cheaper, more efficient. Ben asked Ted what that kind of work had been like.

"Enormously exciting," replied Ted. "Nuclear explosions may not happen anywhere in the universe except where people have learned to make bombs. At Los Alamos, we were working with the most potent known force in the universe."

Ben asked why he had stopped making bombs.

Ted answered, "The question is why would anyone spend their time working on trying to kill as many people as possible? My parents, who didn't like what I was doing, kept asking me that. I would always answer that by making these bombs so destructive, we were making war meaningless. I

thought that governments would never want to have a war when such dangerous weapons existed. But then the Korean War broke out in 1950 and proved me quite wrong. Even though no nuclear weapons were used in Korea, it was clear that their existence had not prevented a war. So I quit Los Alamos. Even then I felt that I had been doing something I would eventually wish I hadn't done."

"Really?" Ben asked. "You regretted it?"

"Yes," said Ted. "Even in those days. I certainly regret it now. I wish I'd spent my time doing something more constructive."

Ted Taylor, along with his associates at Nova, Inc., is doing something more constructive now. They are helping the people of Greenport to solve their water problem. In the kitchen at the home of some Greenport friends, Ted explained to Ben how to get fresh water from salt water. One way is how the *Mimi*'s crew got it—through evaporation.

Water that is heated sufficiently evaporates, or turns to steam, a gas. When the steam cools, it condenses back into water droplets. Condensed water is pure because, as it evaporates, it leaves behind minerals, such as salt.

Another way to purify water is to partly freeze it into a sort of slush, and then let it drain. Ted showed Ben this method in the kitchen. Ted mixed a quart of water with about the same amount of salt as in a quart of sea water. He also added some food coloring to represent any impurities in the water. Then he put a pan of the mixture into the freezer and explained what would happen.

"When water freezes, its *molecules* bond together in crystal shapes. These ice crystals are very fussy about letting any other kind of molecule in. So when the crystals come together, everything that's not a water molecule is pushed out—food coloring, pesticides, salt, pollutants."

"So that's how you're making fresh water from salt water?" asked Ben. "By freezing it?"

"Exactly," said Ted.

A couple of hours later, Ted and Ben took the experimental mixture out of the freezer so that Ben could see if the process worked. The mixture was not completely frozen—it was more like a slush. Ted spooned the slush into a strainer and let it melt and drain into a cup for a while. The result was dramatic. The food coloring and the salt had left the ice and drained into the cup. Ben tasted the remaining mound of ice. This mixture that had been red and salty now was clear and tasted just like normal water.

Ted explained that draining is an essential part of the sequence. This way all the impurities that stick to the sides of the pure ice crystals can be rinsed away by partial melting. He also reminded Ben that, although the process works in a kitchen, he wasn't yet sure that it would work on a scale big enough to provide drinking water for Greenport. Such a scale would require a pile of ice 30 to 40 feet high, not just a couple of inches high.

As seen in the photo on the preceding page, the food coloring and the salt drain out of the ice and into the cup. The ice that remains from the red, salty mixture tastes pure.

In any scientific experiment it is possible to make an error in method or in observation. To try to avoid such errors, scientists repeat an experiment many times. If they get the same results often enough, their conclusions are probably correct. See if you can duplicate the results of the fresh water experiment. Mix a quart of tap water, 3 tablespoons of salt, and some food coloring. Fill an ice tray with the mixture and put it in the freezer compartment of the refrigerator. Leave it for about 3 hours or until the mixture is slush. Fit a large strainer over a glass container and then fill the strainer with slush. Let the slush drain into the glass for at least 20 minutes. What are the results of your experiment? Do they match the results Ted and Ben got? What should your next step be if the results do not match? If they do match?

In your own words, state the problem that you put to the test in this experiment.

Sea water is pumped through the blue pipe you see in the picture above. It is pumped directly to the sprinklers in the Greenport ice pond, shown on the right. Freezing happens naturally in the cold, winter air.

A few hundred yards from Long Island Sound, on a vacant lot, the Village of Greenport has dug a pit 3 feet deep and 70 feet square. Ted doesn't just fill the pit with water and wait for it to freeze. That would take too long, because only the surface of the pond water would be in contact with the cold air. Instead, water is pumped from the sea through a pipe and then sprayed into the air through powerful hoses. Water cools very quickly when it is broken up into droplets of spray.

Like the crew of the *Mimi*, Ted lets nature do much of the work for him. His project can operate only when the temperature falls below 29° Fahrenheit, the point at which salt water begins to freeze. If Greenport had to pay for electricity to freeze the water droplets, then the fresh water from this whole process would cost five or six times the amount people are willing to pay for fresh water. Ted can make a ton of ice for 20 cents or less.

At the bottom of the pond there's a drain that lets the really salty water back out into the sea. When what's left in the pond is drinkable, the drain is closed. Then all the pure ice can melt and the fresh water can go into the Greenport water system.

To see if the freezing and draining process had worked, Ted and Ben waded out into the middle of the pond and gathered a sample of slush. They took it to a nearby shed to test its salt content. Sea water contains 30,000 parts per million (ppm) of salt. The standard for drinking water in New York State allows 400 ppm of salt. For Ted's project to be successful, the salt level of the sea water must be reduced to at least 400 parts per million.

Ben and Ted tested their sample from the pond with a *salinity meter*. Ben poured the water in and pressed a button on the meter. The dial moved only to 35. Because 35 ppm is less than a tenth of the salt allowed in New York State drinking water, this meant that Ted's pond is very successful! Ben tasted the water, which was probably purer than the drinking water in most towns.

Greenport was using simple technology to solve its water supply problem by purifying sea water cheaply. Ben realized similar projects might also be used in a lot of other towns located in cold regions.

"Does this project have anything to do with your regretting that you worked on the bomb?"

"It sure does," admitted Ted. "About 10 years ago, I decided that I wanted to work only on things that would be interesting and fun to do, and that would make life better for people instead of more dangerous. Working on ice ponds is just as much fun as any of the other projects I've been involved in. And it certainly is of more benefit to people than atomic bombs are. I chose to work on this project because I thought it was a good example of a different role for technology, something on a small scale. Science doesn't have to be big to make sense."

THE FEAST

The next morning, both Rachel and Arthur checked the water supply and made a welcome discovery. A major problem had been solved.

"And we were worried about whether the stills could make enough fresh water for us to survive," Rachel said wryly.

"Well, we didn't know it was going to rain last night," replied Arthur.

Rachel grinned. "Now the stills are *reservoirs*."

"Come and get it!" Ramon shouted, when breakfast was ready.

C.T. was the last to arrive. "I didn't think **you'd** miss breakfast," Ramon said to the boy. "Where have you been?"

C.T. turned and proudly pointed at his morning's work. An American flag hung upside down from a tree at the edge of the woods.

Captain Granville smiled at his grandson. "Good work, son," he said.

But Arthur was puzzled. "The flag's upside down, C.T."

"Flying the flag upside down is a distress signal. Grandpa told me."

Nobody was very pleased with the breakfast menu.

"Two bites and breakfast will be over," sighed Arthur.

"We have to cut way back," Ramon explained. "We left port with only five days of rations."

"Well, it's pretty obvious," Anne concluded, "that we're going to have to **find** our food somehow."

Arthur was doubtful. "On this rock? Starvation city, man!"

"There's always the ocean," Sally Ruth pointed out.

Ramon was enthusiastic. "That's right. We should start fishing!"

"Ramon," Rachel said grinning, "if we have to count on your fishing, we'd better get rescued by lunchtime."

"We can gather things from the shore while the tide's out," Sally Ruth offered.

C.T. held out a handful of strawberries. "It's a good thing I found these."

The group fanned out to gather the bounty of their uninhabited "rock."

Arthur and C.T. collected plants and berries. C.T. knew just what to look for.

"Beach peas — you cook them like garden peas," he told Arthur. "Milkweed — tastes like broccoli."

"How do you know all this?" Arthur asked, impressed.

"Mom taught me," C.T. answered. "She knows all about wild edible plants. You've got to watch out, though," he warned, pointing to a purple flower. "Some plants are edible, but **all** irises are poisonous."

"Hey, how about this?" Arthur called, pointing to a mushroom.

"Don't touch it," C.T. said. "I don't know if it's poisonous or not. But the rule is, if you don't know exactly what it is, don't touch it and don't eat it."

Meanwhile, the others foraged along the shoreline and in the *tidepools*.

Rachel showed Sally Ruth and Ramon her catch. "Mussels and clams! We're going to have a feast!" she exclaimed.

"Uh . . . that's great, Rachel," Ramon said reluctantly, "but I'm afraid we can't use them."

"The red tide," Sally Ruth added. "Your shellfish could be poisonous."

Rachel didn't understand. "The water isn't red here. And I've eaten shellfish I've gathered myself lots of times. Nothing ever happened!"

"That's because those beaches had been checked," Ramon explained.

"And the water doesn't have to look red," Sally Ruth added.

Ramon went on. "It's called the red tide because sometimes, not always, it makes the water kind of reddish. The red tide is a *micro-algae* that clams and mussels and oysters eat. It doesn't hurt them — but it can kill humans who eat shellfish that have eaten the algae. Red tide is most likely to happen in spring and summer. We don't know if these waters have the algae or not."

Rachel nodded. "Guess we can't take the chance," she sighed, dumping out her bucketful of shellfish.

Before long, Sally Ruth found something that made up for the loss, and she held it high in the air.

"Lobster!" Ramon cried.

"Is that safe to eat?" Rachel asked.

"Yep," Ramon replied. "Lobsters don't eat the dangerous algae."

Meanwhile, C.T. continued to search for food in the woods . . . while Arthur returned to camp to work on their communications problem.

"Arthur, you're taking apart your radio?" Rachel asked.

"I have to," Arthur replied sadly. "I've got to see if I can find the parts to fix the transmitter on the VHF."

C.T. returned to camp with a knapsack of good things to eat. He had cow parsnip, reindeer moss, red clover, dandelion greens, and meat.

"What is . . . what was that?" Arthur asked.

"A rabbit," C.T. said. "I trapped it — set a snare. It's great to eat."

Everyone except Rachel was impressed. "Ugh! Gross!" she exploded. "C.T., look at all this other food. You didn't have to kill a poor rabbit!"

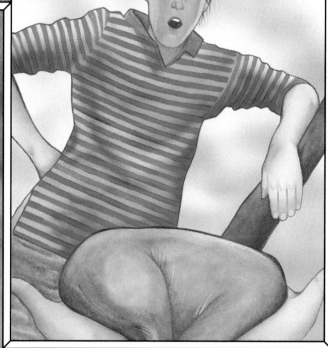

"Hey, I didn't know we'd find all these other things," C.T. retorted. "All I knew was that we needed food badly. I got us some. Rabbit meat is food."

Rachel was unconvinced. "Rabbits can think! People keep rabbits as pets – they don't have pet lobsters!"

Arthur interrupted. "Rachel, there's a guy I know in Brooklyn who has a pet snail. Calls it John Travolta. Dude's kind of weird, though . . . ."

C.T.'s feelings were hurt. "I caught this for everybody. It wasn't easy."

"Fine," Rachel countered, "but I'm not eating it."

"You eat hamburgers, don't you?" C.T. asked. "Hot dogs? Fried chicken? Steak? Pork chops?"

"Okay, okay," Rachel admitted, "but I don't go out and kill the living things they come from."

"Somebody has to," Arthur pointed out quietly. "Everything has to live off something else that lives."

Rachel hesitated. "I . . . I don't know. I have to think about this," she said.

"Well, you sure don't want to do it on an empty stomach," Anne added with a smile. "Let's get cooking!"

Everyone pitched in to prepare the feast. When it was ready, they gathered at the table. Anne looked at the food spread before them and shook her head in amazement. "Imagine, every single thing here was gathered with our own hands."

They all dug in hungrily. They sampled the seaweed, munched the berries, and chomped salad greens. They compared the flavor of the lobster and the rabbit.

Rachel watched the others enjoying the rabbit meat. Finally, she spoke up. "Listen, C.T.," she said warmly, "I'm sorry I got so bent out of shape before. It is pretty amazing that you caught that thing."

"It's okay," he said shyly. "Thanks."

The Captain cleared his throat. "There's something I'd like to say," he began. "This is one fine meal. And if it weren't for you, I wouldn't be here to enjoy it. You saved my life and my boat. I don't know which I value more."

He raised his glass in a toast. "You're as fine and brave a crew as ever I put to sea with," he concluded.

There was a moment of silence, while everyone savored the Captain's words. Then Ramon spoke. "We're glad you pulled through, Captain." Turning to the others, he shouted, "We're glad we all pulled through!"

"Here's to Captain Granville," Anne said. They cheered and raised their glasses.

So the feast went on as the afternoon sun dipped slowly toward the horizon. Some obstacles remained for the castaways. But now they felt that they were a family as well as a crew.

How Does it Get There?

On Seal Island, the castaways search for, gather, and prepare all the food they put on their plates. They discover that there is more to the story of food than what ends up on the dinner table. As Arthur points out, "Everything has to live off something else that lives." In fact, every living thing is part of a food chain with many links. One way to describe a food chain is the route by which food travels to your plate.

What are the links in your food chain?

1. List everything you ate for lunch yesterday.
2. Choose one food and find out all the ingredients of that food.
3. Trace each ingredient back to its source. For example, if you ate a hamburger, ask yourself these questions:
   • What is the main ingredient of a hamburger?
   • What is the source of this ingredient?
   • What food did the source eat?
   • What did the source's food need to live?

Your answers will show each link in one of the food chains that make up your diet. Trace some other foods in your lunch.
4. What can you say about where all food chains begin?
5. Based on your research, how might Rachel feel about eating your lunch?

A NEW ALCHEMY

When the members of the *Mimi* crew found themselves on a remote island without enough food, they faced a big problem: survival. They solved that problem because they had special knowledge. C.T. knew which kinds of wild plants are edible and knew how to snare a rabbit. Ramon and Sally Ruth knew which sea plants and animals are edible. As a result, they had plenty to eat. In fact, they had a feast. Their special knowledge made them self-sufficient and saved their lives.

At the New Alchemy Institute in East Falmouth, Massachusetts, some people have developed that kind of self-sufficiency for everyday life. They run a small farm. It is a kind of laboratory in which they experiment with natural methods of growing food. Greg Watson is one of those people. He is a science teacher and environmental expert who has worked at New Alchemy for four years.

Mark Graham, who plays Arthur in "The Voyage of the *Mimi*," visited Greg Watson at the New Alchemy Institute. Greg gave Mark a kind of working tour of the institute, starting at "Compost City."

Compost is plant matter that is decaying, or rotting. Compost decays because tiny organisms feed on it. Eventually, their fertile waste material is all that's left in the form of good, nutrient-rich soil.

The structure of the geodesic dome uses two important principles of geometry: a sphere and a triangle. A sphere incorporates a maximum amount of inside space with a minimum amount of surface area. A triangle is the only polygon that is rigid and can hold its shape. The geodesic dome is a very strong structure built with little material.

All the dead leaves, flowers, fruits, and vegetables from New Alchemy's gardens get dumped into bins at Compost City. By providing lots of air, water, and nitrogen (in the form of manure), the New Alchemists speed up the composting process. They can make a pile of dead plants into living soil in a matter of weeks. This process takes nature a year or more

It is this basic process, Greg explained, that gave New Alchemy its name. In medieval Europe, an alchemist was a person who tried to turn lead, a worthless substance, into gold, a valuable substance. To most people, dead, rotting plants are useless garbage. To the New Alchemists they are the first step in growing healthy, delicious food.

In a one-acre garden, the New Alchemist gardeners grow everything from broccoli to grapes. The gardeners never need chemical fertilizers or insecticides. They have studied nature's ways and copy them. For instance, they copy nature's way of protecting soil. When it rains, topsoil can be washed off garden beds. This wash-off doesn't happen in a forest because a natural cover of dead leaves protects the soil. New Alchemy gardeners lay down a cover of "mulch"—dead leaves or straw or dried sea-

Tilapia are well suited for fish-farming because they thrive in warm water and are delicious to eat. Their wastes add nitrogen to the water, which is then used to irrigate and fertilize greenhouse plants.

weed. Mulch protects the soil, keeps roots moist longer, and actually fertilizes as it decays. Mark helped lay down such a cover during his working tour.

The New Alchemy outdoor garden flourishes from May through October. But the farmers grow food all year long, even in Massachusetts where it snows much of the winter. They grow it in "season-extending cold frames." These are plastic domes that cover small garden beds. The domes trap light, heat, and moisture while protecting the plants from chilly air or wind. The gardeners have also built a number of solar greenhouses called bioshelters. The bioshelters have clear plastic ceilings and walls that allow sunlight to enter. They contain huge tubs (300 to 600 gallons) of water that trap and store heat from the sun. Lots of fruits and vegetables grow year round in this warm, steamy environment.

*Geese mow the lawn and
help fertilize the grass.*

New Alchemists are solar farmers. So, they never have to pay fuel bills for their greenhouses. Their gardens won't die if there's a sudden fuel shortage or if the heating system breaks down. The sun shines all year round.

But the sun doesn't shine at night. So, the New Alchemists have again copied nature. During the day the world's oceans and lakes absorb heat slowly, retain it for a while, and release it slowly. Similarly, the huge tubs in the greenhouses absorb and store the heat of the sun. The tubs are also the home for great schools of *tilapia,* hardy tropical fish that taste delicious.

Growing fish in a closed environment, such as a greenhouse tub, presents problems. In a river or lake, there is an exchange of water: oxygen flows in and wastes flow out. Without this exchange of water, fish and other life would die. So at New Alchemy, lots of algae are grown in the tubs. These plants absorb the fish wastes as fertilizer and give off oxygen that the fish breathe. Also, the solar farmers occasionally change part of the water in the tubs.

During the day he spent at the New Alchemy Institute, Mark learned many things. For one, he learned it is a pleasure to come out of the cold and into a greenhouse. Melons, tomatoes, greens, even figs and kumquats grow in the warm climate. In the greenhouse, he was able to pick his lunch. And the leftovers on his plate went into the compost bin where the life process starts all over again.

With knowledge, hard work, and some money to get started, the average family can do what the New Alchemists have done. One tenth of one acre of land, if planted and fertilized properly, will provide three vegetable servings each day, year round, for 13 people. The smallest greenhouse at New Alchemy was built for less than $2,000. It provides vegetables for four people, year round, with no expense other than seeds and garden tools.

Grow your own! Buy some sunflower seeds in a food store, and plant them in a tall, wide can. Here's how. Punch 3 holes in the bottom of the can. Cover the inside bottom with ½ inch of pebbles for water drainage. Fill ¾ full with rich soil. Remove the hulls from a couple of sunflower seeds. Toss the seeds in the can and add more soil to fill the can. Put the can in a drain dish—a pie tin will do. Then put the whole thing on a windowsill that gets plenty of sun. Water heavily three times a week. Start planting in early summer, and by September you should see a tall flower. Many seeds are produced by one sunflower, which is really dozens of flowers bunched together on a disk.

Check the fruit bowl and vegetable bin at home, and experiment with growing other plants from seeds.

ROLLING HOME

The sound of the ax hitting the wood echoed across Seal Island. Anne labored to chop down a tall, straight tree to use as the *Mimi's* new bowsprit.

Meanwhile, C.T. had found an empty bottle with a cork in it. Sitting on the rocks overlooking the cove, he wrote a note on a scrap of paper:

DEAR FINDER
WE HAVE BEEN STUCK FOR
FIVE DAYS ON SEAL ISLAND AT
43°53 NORTH 68°45 WEST
WE ARE TRYING TO GET OFF.
IF YOU FIND THIS MESSAGE
CHECK WITH THE COAST GUARD
TO SEE IF WE GOT OFF OKAY
IF WE DIDNT COME GET US.
THIS IS NOT A JOKE

C.T.
GRANVILLE ℅ MIMI
P.S. MY HOME TOWN IS GIBBUN
VILLE OHIO

He added the date, pulled the cork out of the bottle and put the note inside. After replacing the cork, he tossed the bottle far out into the water. His small cry for help was adrift in the vast ocean.

In the forest, the tree was ready to fall. "TIMBERRR!" Anne shouted as it crashed to the ground.

When all the branches had been trimmed from the felled tree, the crew members hauled it to the beach. There, under Captain Granville's direction, they began the long, hard task of fashioning a new bowsprit for the crippled *Mimi.*

As the work on the bowsprit progressed, C.T. kept track of the passing days. Around a tiny pine tree he placed a circle of stones to represent a calendar. There was a stone for each day spent on the island.

Over the next five days, work on the bowsprit occupied most of everyone's time and energy.

The two pieces of the old bowsprit were measured to determine the correct length.

The bark was stripped from the tree, exposing the hard surface of the wood. The log was smoothed and shaped, and all knots and bumps were chiseled away.

One end of the log was cut to fit the iron collar in which the *Mimi*'s rigging would be secured to the bowsprit. The other end was shaped to fit through the *gunnel* into brackets on the *prow*.

Finally, to make it stronger and seal it against water and weather, the now smooth log was coated with *pitch*.

Arthur continued to work on the radio. The castaways could receive radio transmissions, but still could not send transmissions. They knew a search was under way for them, but they had no way to let the Coast Guard know where they were.

It was the eighth night on the island. Sally Ruth was tending the fire, while others were crowded into the shelter. C.T. was studying the navigation charts.

"There are more than three thousand islands off the coast of Maine," he announced.

"Looking for us is like looking for a needle in a haystack," Rachel said with a sigh. She turned to Arthur, who was tinkering with the radio. "Have you listened for our whale lately?" she asked.

"Every now and then," Arthur replied, "but I'm afraid that whale is long gone." Suddenly, he had an idea. "Rachel, turn on the whale tag receiver." With the receiver on, Arthur took two wires from the radio transmitter and touched them together.

Bzzt----bzzt!

"Hey, do that again!" Rachel said. "The receiver is picking you up!"

"Can you transmit?" the Captain asked.

Arthur shrugged. "Within four feet."

"Turn on the emergency frequency—channel sixteen," Captain Granville said.

"Try an S.O.S.," added Rachel, excitedly. "Three shorts, three longs, three shorts. That's all the Morse Code I know."

Arthur touched the two wires together to tap out the code. S.O.S...:S.O.S....S.O.S...., over and over again.

Everyone waited and hoped.

"Well, it isn't working," the Captain concluded. "Maybe . . ."

He was interrupted by the crackling sound of the receiver, and then . . .

"This is the Coast Guard. We copy an S.O.S. from an unidentified source. Can you give us name and location? Over."

Pandemonium broke loose. Everyone in the shelter spoke at once. But no one there knew enough Morse Code to send the Coast Guard accurate information.

"I'll go get Sally Ruth," Anne said as she headed out of the shelter. "She knows Morse Code."

Sally Ruth was just as excited as the others. Using the makeshift transmitter, she tapped out the message: "This is the *Mimi* calling."

The Coast Guard's reply came quickly. "We copy you, *Mimi*. We've been looking for you. Can you tell us your location and status? Over."

Sally Ruth transmitted their location, and confirmed that they were all okay. The Coast Guard was ready to send a helicopter to take them off the island, to the delight of the crew. But Captain Granville had a better idea.

"Hold it," he said, interrupting the cheers. "We don't have to have the Coast Guard come get us. The *Mimi*'s almost fixed. We can rescue ourselves."

The Captain's idea was accepted unanimously.

"But shouldn't we have the Coast Guard contact our parents so they won't worry?" Rachel asked.

Sally Ruth tapped out the message. She instructed the Coast Guard to contact Erik who could notify the families of everyone on the *Mimi*.

The next day everyone worked especially hard to finish the bowsprit. Taking a break from their work, the Captain and crew posed for a picture to commemorate their stay on Seal Island. Sally Ruth aimed and focused the camera and set the automatic timer. Then she rushed to take her place with the others before the shutter clicked.

The final step in repairing the *Mimi* began. The crew floated the new bowsprit out to the boat, hoisted it with a block and tackle, and bolted it in place. Under Captain Granville's supervision, the rigging was run through the collar.

"Make sure you get that collar tight," he cautioned. "I don't want any more unexpected cold baths. Falling overboard once is enough for me."

When the work was completed, everyone admired the new bowsprit.

"I think we've got ourselves a boat again," the Captain said. "My guess is she'll sail as good as new. Good work."

In the late afternoon, Captain Granville and Sally Ruth were returning from the *Mimi*. Sally Ruth stepped out of the dory into the shallow water to pull the boat into shore. Suddenly, she lost her balance and fell with a loud splash. The Captain, still sitting in the dory, gave a loud hoot and teased her.

Laughing, Sally Ruth responded by pushing the Captain out of the boat and into the water.

From the beach, the others laughed at the drenched pair. That was all it took for Captain Granville and Sally Ruth to team up. Scooping up mud from the bottom, they hurled it at the jeering group on the shore. And a glorious mud battle was under way. All the pent-up tension of the past week was released in a loud, laughing, happy free-for-all with Seal Island goo.

Later that evening, happy and exhausted, the group sat around the campfire.

Captain Granville played his guitar and sang an old sea chanty. The crew joined in the chorus:

"Ten long days upon this island,
Driven by the wind and storm,
We found food and we found water,
Made a shelter snug and warm.
Rolling home, rolling home,
Rolling home across the sea.
Rolling home to old New England,
Rolling home, dear land, to thee . . . ."

The next morning, it was time to break camp. The castaways took down the shelter and the solar stills. They packed up their gear and loaded it back onto the *Mimi*. They scattered the cold ashes from their campfire and collected all the trash. The ten stones placed in a circle were left as evidence of their island adventure.

Captain Granville waited in the cove with the dory as C.T. took care of one final chore. The boy climbed the tree and removed the American flag that had been their distress signal during those anxious days. Then he and his grandfather rowed out to the *Mimi*, C.T.'s voice floating out over the cove:

"Rolling home, rolling home . . .
Rolling home
across the sea . . . ."

Dot's It!

Below is the Morse Code alphabet of dots and dashes used by ships all over the world.

A •—	H ••••	O ———	U ••—
B —•••	I ••	P •——•	V •••—
C —•—•	J •———	Q ——•—	W •——
D —••	K —•—	R •—•	X —••—
E •	L •—••	S •••	Y —•——
F ••—•	M ——	T —	Z ——••
G ——•	N —•		

Use the Morse Code alphabet to decode the following message:

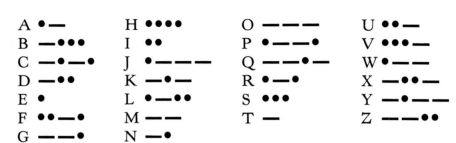

Use sound or light to help Sally Ruth transmit the following message to the Coast Guard:

MIMI AND CREW ALL O.K. DON'T SEND CHOPPER. SHIP FIXED. WE WILL RESCUE OURSELVES.

Send and Receive

Here is the key to another code called Pigpen:

The symbol for each letter of the alphabet is the part of the diagram where it appears. For example:

H = ⊓   J = >   R = ⊡   Z = ⋀

Use Pigpen to send the following message:

WATER, WATER EVERYWHERE NOR ANY DROP TO DRINK.

Captain Coleridge of the *Ancient Mariner*

Use Pigpen to receive the following message:

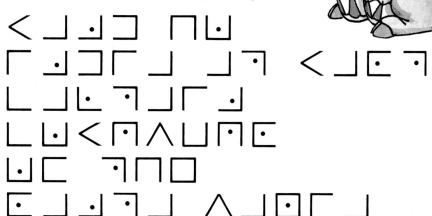

Where in the World?

9/19/84

S.O.S. Marooned on Ragged Island. 43° 50'N Latitude, 68° 57'W Longitude. Need food, water, and medical supplies.

Captain Ahab of the Pequod

HINT: USE YOUR WALL CHART TO HELP YOU.

If you found these notes in bottles floating in the ocean, where in the world would you have to go to rescue each writer?

Now it's your turn. Pretend you need help. Write a note giving your exact location, including latitude and longitude. Decide the best way to send your S.O.S. out into the world.

September, Full Moon

Help! Ship wrecked in hurricane. Adrift 22 days. No food. Land ahead at 42° 30'N Latitude, 42° E Longitude. Situation desperate.

Captain Jason of the Argo

HINT: USE A WORLD ATLAS TO HELP YOU.

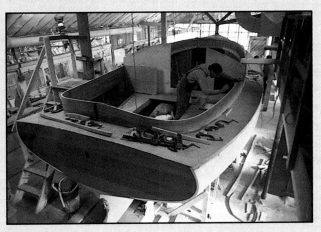

Stuck on an island without many tools, the *Mimi*'s crew found that it was difficult to build a new bowsprit. But by following a plan and measuring carefully, the crew managed pretty well. Building a whole boat is not so different. Boat builders have to follow a pattern and measure carefully. To find out more about building boats, Mark Graham visited the Landing Boatshop in Kennebunkport, Maine.

The boatshop is located on the Kennebunk River. About 150 years ago, there were many boat builders along the river. When a ship was launched and maneuvered down the river to the Atlantic Ocean, there was great excitement. In the 1850s, the boat-building industry started to die out until, finally, there were no boats launched on the Kennebunk at all. But in 1978, a new 14-foot rowboat was slipped into the river. It had been built by students at the Landing Boatshop.

The boatshop has two programs: boat design and boat building. Each program has about 15 students who study for at least one year. Mark visited the design room first.

During the course of a year, each student in this program designs four boats: a sailboat, a motorboat, a commercial workboat (such as a tug or trawler), and a fourth boat of the student's choice. Designing a boat requires some pretty complicated mathematics. Students must figure out how much sail or engine power their boats will need, and how to make their boats float.

Mark learned that boats float by displacing water. Take the *Mimi* as an example. Imagine that she's floating in a big tank of water, and then the water freezes solid all around her. Then imagine that you can lift the *Mimi* right out of the tank, leaving a big hole in the ice where she was. Then imagine that you filled that hole with water. If you could weigh the water, you would find that the amount it took to fill the hole weighed 50 tons. That's also how much the *Mimi* weighs. So, in order to float, she has to displace 50 tons of water.

Not every object can float when placed in water. A 50-ton steel ball, for instance, would sink immediately if placed in a tank of water. This would happen because the weight of a steel ball is compressed into a small area. In order for an object to float, its weight has to be spread out. Thus, the greater the weight of a boat, the longer or wider the boat must be.

As Mark walked around the design room, he got to meet some of the students and look at their drawings. One student he met was Deborah Scaling. She has an interesting reason for being in the design program at the Landing Boatshop.

Debbie is a world-class sailor who has been sailing since she was eight years old. Now she is 25 years old, and she has sailed to Europe, Africa, South America and Australia. She was a member of the first all-women crew to race a 65-foot boat across the Atlantic. Sailing is her life, she told Mark. She joined the design program to design safer boats because, about a year earlier, she was in a serious boating accident. She and four friends were sailing a boat from Maine to Florida. Off the coast of North Carolina, they ran into a bad storm.

"We had winds from eighty to a hundred knots and seas from thirty-five to fifty feet. We were in a

Students in the design program, like Debbie Scaling, study math in order to design safe boats.

boat that was very heavy, and had great big cabin windows. The combination of all that weight and those big cabin windows was disastrous. The boat was picked up on a huge wave that broke right under it. The boat was smacked down on its side and all the windows caved in. Before the boat could stand back up again, it was filled with water and going under.

"Where were you at the time?" asked Mark.

"I was asleep in a bunk," said Debbie. "I'd been at the helm for thirteen hours, and I just couldn't stay up any longer. Just before the boat sank, we managed to get out of it and into a little dinghy we had on board. For five days my friends and I floated around out in the Atlantic. There were sharks all around us and, because it was cold, three of the people got hypothermia. They died. After five days a Russian freighter rescued us. The Russians brought us to land and my friend and I recuperated in a hospital for a few days. I don't want anyone else to have to go through what my friends and I went through, so I'm here to learn to design safer boats."

Mark was stunned by Debbie's story. It made him appreciate the design program, and all the thought and care that goes into planning a safe boat.

Experiment with sinking objects. Pour water into a ½-liter measuring cup up to the 350-ml mark. Find a small stone that you can hold in the palm of your hand, and gently drop it into the cup. What happened to the stone? Why? What happened to the water? How much water did the stone displace?

Experiment with other objects. Predict whether each will sink or float in water and test your prediction.

Wood from Ward Allen's lumber mill is steamed (middle photo) and pressed into the boat mold while still hot (right photo). Then the wood is clamped (photo below) so it will dry permanently bent.

Before good designs can become safe boats, the builders need wood. The boatshop buys special wood, such as teak and mahogany, from dealers who import it from around the world. But most of their pine and oak comes from a local sawmill. Mark visited the sawmill with some of the boatshop's instructors who personally inspect the wood to make sure the grain is straight. Mark helped cut down a tree, and then watched as it came out of the sawmill in smooth, white boards.

Back at the boatshop, Mark learned what happens to those smooth boards. First they have to be cut to size to fit the shape of a boat, which is very curved in some places. Then the cut wood, which will be the ribs of the boat, has to be bent. The process of steaming softens wood and makes it easy to bend. So, the ribs are heated for about an hour in a steamer. When the ribs come out, the builders have to work fast to get them in place before they can cool and begin to dry. If too much time is taken, the ribs crack when bent. Once pressed into place, the ribs are clamped and screwed down until they dry in this bent position.

Mark was sorry to leave Kennebunkport before any of the boats he had seen were completed. The school finishes several boats a year, from 12-foot dories to 30-foot sailboats. They are all launched in the Kennebunk River, and the launching is celebrated with a party. After seeing all the work that goes into making a boat, Mark could understand why the boat builders would want to throw a party. After all, he remembered how happy the folks on the *Mimi* had been when they finished building just a bowsprit.

SEPARATE WAYS

The day was clear and bright when the *Mimi* set out from Seal Island. Rachel, Sally Ruth, Arthur, and Ramon looked back as the island's rocky shoreline receded into the distance.

"Feels like leaving home," Arthur sighed. "I'm going to miss it."

"That island really took good care of us," Rachel said wistfully.

"We took care of ourselves, too," Ramon added.

Anne was at the wheel. Nearby, C.T. was working on his nautical chart.

"The new course line?" Anne asked. C.T. nodded.

"What did you write on the chart for the last ten days?" Anne wondered.

"Just 'shipwrecked,'" C.T. replied. "I don't have enough room for everything that happened."

"What you need is a journal."

When the others had gone below, Ramon said to Anne, "I hate to see this expedition end."

Anne frowned and said, "I finally get my research grant, and look what

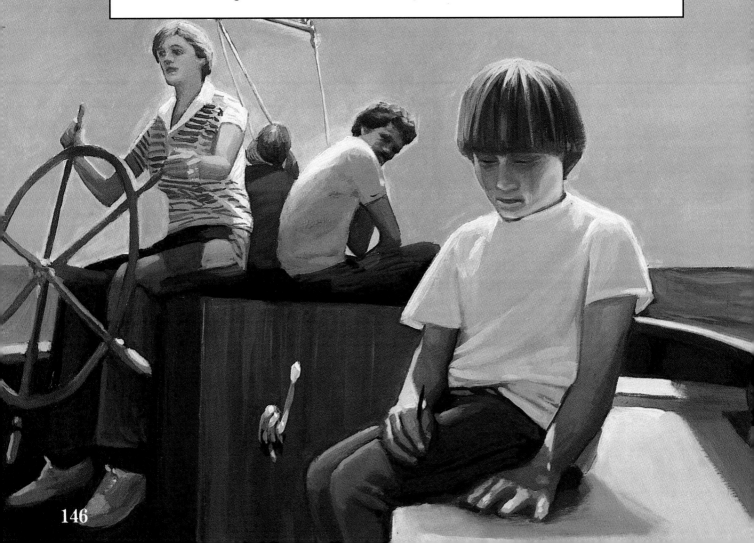

happens. We stop data collection a month early. I almost get everybody killed. I lose an expensive radio tag. And . . ."

"Whoa!" Ramon interrupted her. "Wait a minute! We gathered a ton of data that we still have to analyze. We have census figures, fluke IDs, behavior observations, a day and a half of close observations on the radio tag . . ."

"Which almost got us wrecked," Anne interjected.

Ramon looked at her impatiently. "So, you take credit for the storm, too? Don't forget, this group you led survived that storm, and we made it through ten days on a remote island, fending for ourselves."

"Ramon," Anne said, convinced at last, "I like the way you describe things."

The scientific work continued as the *Mimi* headed back to port. Rachel and Anne studied the water temperature information Rachel had gathered with the bathythermographs. In the saloon, Arthur and Sally Ruth sorted the fluke photos.

"Arthur, look at this!" Sally Ruth exclaimed suddenly.

A few minutes later, they called Ramon and Sally Ruth handed him one of the fluke photos.

"It's Crystal," Ramon said.

"Right," Sally Ruth confirmed. "That was Crystal in 1980 and this is Crystal in 1982," she said, handing him a second photo.

Ramon looked puzzled.

"It's the same whale in both photos," Arthur assured him.

Sally Ruth explained. "The scars are alike, but the black and white patterns are different."

"Here's another one that's changed," Arthur said, handing over two more photos. "Epaulet, in 1980 and in 1981."

"*Incredible!*" Ramon muttered in Spanish. "They've changed! The patterns are never supposed to change, and yet they've changed!"

"Over a couple of years, you could mistake the changed patterns for different whales," Arthur pointed out.

"This is an important discovery you guys made," Ramon announced.

"Sally Ruth made the discovery," Arthur noted.

"We both did," Sally Ruth insisted.

"It's unbelievable!" Ramon said, still amazed. And he left to gather the rest of the fluke photos.

"I'm going to get some music," Arthur said, turning on the radio.

"Just don't play it too loud," Sally Ruth joked, heading for the fo'c'sle.

"Hey," Arthur said, "that sounds like the radio tag!" and he raised the volume on the receiver. But the red blip on the ADF screen continued to move and the sound was gone.

"Guess not," Arthur concluded, and went to help with the sails.

As Sally Ruth passed through the galley a little later, the ADF screen caught her eye. The red blip was no longer moving: the ADF had locked onto the signal from the radio tag.

C.T. took the wheel while the others gathered around the ADF to hear the telltale signal.

Captain Granville said, "Do you think it's still attached to the whale?"

"No," Ramon assured him. "It probably fell off days ago. The signal isn't constant because sometimes it's blocked by the waves."

"Let's pick it up," the Captain said, and he called up to C.T. "Mr. Granville! Will you come right 15 degrees, please!"

"Aye-aye, Cap'n," the boy called back, turning the wheel to the new heading.

Guided by the ADF, the *Mimi* soon came upon the red and white whale tag, bobbing in the waves. Ramon scooped it up with a long-handled net.

"Hey, Ramon! You finally caught something!" Rachel called out.

Then the boat was back on course and at the dock in Gloucester almost before the crew knew it. The voyage of the *Mimi* was over.

Everyone hurried to the telephones. After calling his own family, Arthur sent a telegram that Sally Ruth dictated in sign language:

SAFE ON SHORE. STOP. HOME IN WEEK. STOP. WILL WRITE TONIGHT. STOP. LOVE, SALLY RUTH

And Rachel meant it when she said, "Mom, it's great to hear your voice."

C.T. had the biggest surprise of all. His parents had been away all week and didn't even know about the shipwreck!

Then the crew gathered at the dock to say goodbye. Anne spoke first. "I have a few things to say. Mostly, I want to congratulate you all. Despite all our problems, we still learned a lot."

"We learned that Captain Granville can sing," Ramon joked.

"And that Arthur can't," Rachel added.

Anne laughed. "Seriously," she said, "we did learn a lot about whales."

"That changing fluke pattern discovery Sally Ruth and Arthur made will really shake up a lot of our fellow whale researchers," said Ramon.

"And Rachel's XBT data are very interesting," Anne continued. "C.T., you were a great help with that project. In fact, I think our work is good enough to get money for another voyage."

"Maybe Greenland next summer," Ramon suggested.

"Hey," Arthur said, "that's great, you guys."

"What do you mean, you guys? Don't you and Rachel want to come?"

Just then, Erik arrived to pick up Anne, Ramon, and Sally Ruth. At the same time, the taxi arrived to take Arthur and Rachel to the bus station.

"Don't say goodbye," Sally Ruth said. And she showed them how to sign the words: Until next time.

After all the hugs and handshakes, Arthur and Rachel climbed into the waiting taxi and left for the bus station.

Anne turned to Captain Granville. "We couldn't have asked for a better captain. Are you free next summer?"

"It would be a pleasure," was the Captain's answer.

"Goodbye, Captain," Sally Ruth said. The Captain replied in sign language: Until next time.

To C.T., Sally Ruth said, "We have something for you."

C.T. opened the box she handed him. "A journal! Thanks!"

"It's from all of us," Anne said. "For your next voyage."

Finally, Captain Granville and C.T. were alone on the dock. "C.T., let's find a nice little restaurant and get some shoreside rations," the Captain said.

"Grandpa," C.T. said, "I think I'd like to be a sailor when I grow up."

"You've had a good start," the Captain replied, a hint of pride in his voice.

"Or a scientist," C.T. added.

"Why not both?"

The Captain put his arm around his grandson's shoulders, as they walked along the dock toward shore.

THE END . . . UNTIL NEXT TIME.

A Voyage of Discoveries

The voyage of the *Mimi* was a voyage full of discoveries about whales, science, math, nature, and people. The pictures on these pages show some of the important things members of the *Mimi* crew learned or discovered. Each line of dialogue belongs to a picture. Try to match each picture with the dialogue.

1. "Those bumps are called tubercles. There's a little stiff hair on each one. The ancestors of whales lived on land, and that's all that's left of their hair."

2. "That's called a breach!"

3. "Captain, I think I've found the problem."

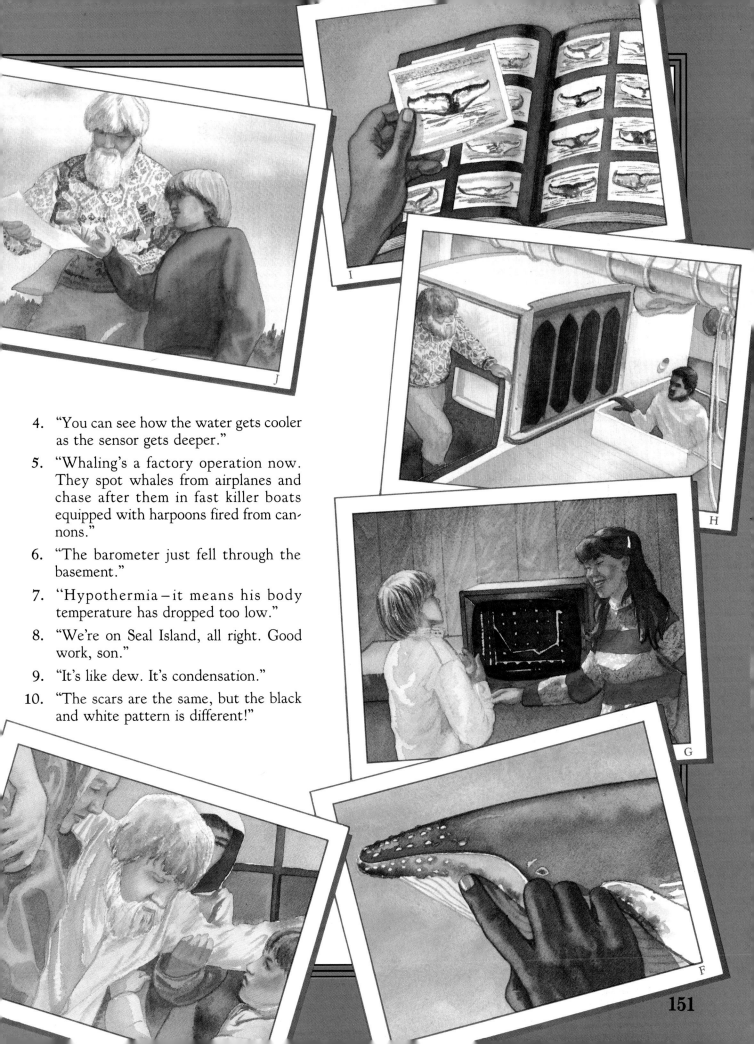

4. "You can see how the water gets cooler as the sensor gets deeper."

5. "Whaling's a factory operation now. They spot whales from airplanes and chase after them in fast killer boats equipped with harpoons fired from cannons."

6. "The barometer just fell through the basement."

7. "Hypothermia—it means his body temperature has dropped too low."

8. "We're on Seal Island, all right. Good work, son."

9. "It's like dew. It's condensation."

10. "The scars are the same, but the black and white pattern is different!"

A SAILOR AND A SCIENTIST

Peter explained to Ben how the earth's magnetic field helps people to navigate with compasses. The two stars of the "The Voyage of the Mimi" were happy to be together again.

I think I'd like to be a sailor when I grow up," C.T. says at the end of the "The Voyage of the *Mimi.*" "Or a scientist."

"Why not both?" Captain Granville asks.

Peter Marston plays Captain Granville, and he actually is both a sailor and a scientist. He really does own the *Mimi,* and he works with magnets and magnetic force at the Massachusetts Institute of Technology (M.I.T.). Ben Affleck visited Peter aboard the *Mimi* in Gloucester, Massachusetts.

Ben went there to learn about magnets. Peter told him that every magnet has two poles, a north pole and a south pole. Peter used small bar magnets to show Ben how magnetic poles work. One magnet's north pole and another magnet's south pole attract each other and stick together. But when one magnet's south pole and another magnet's south pole are put next to each other, they scoot away from each other. In other words, *unlike poles attract and like poles repel.*

"The earth has a north pole and a south pole," said Ben. "That's right," Peter told him. "In fact, the earth itself is a magnet." The earth has a weak magnetic field with poles at the top and bottom. No one quite understands why the earth is magnetic. It is thought that a molten core of iron and nickel at the center of the earth creates the magnetic force.

Because the earth has a magnetic field, people can navigate with compasses. A compass needle itself is a simple bar magnet. The ends of the needle point to their opposite poles, because the earth's

magnetic poles attract them. One end is always attracted to the north and the other to the south.

Peter and Ben left the *Mimi* and went to the lab where Peter works. He works at the Plasma Fusion Center at M.I.T. Peter works there with magnets, but not with the kind he and Ben had been playing with on the boat. Those little magnets are called permanent magnets, and they are always magnetic. Peter works with gigantic electromagnets. They are magnetic only when turned on.

Electromagnets are, basically, coils of wire. When an electric current is sent through the coil, it creates a magnetic field. If a bar of steel is placed in the field, it becomes very strongly magnetized and creates a much stronger field. Ben was surprised at the force of the electromagnet that Peter showed him. The force was so strong that it made a key leap out of Ben's hand when he held it 12 inches away from the magnet. It made Ben's pocket knife stick so tightly that he couldn't pull it off no matter how hard he tried. "Oh, good, another knife for my collection," joked Peter. The knife came free of the magnet only when Peter turned off the electric current.

But even this powerful magnet is small compared to the magnets Peter usually works with. He showed Ben a machine that makes use of gigantic magnets. Peter is part of a team of scientists at M.I.T. who are building this large machine. The scientists hope the machine will create an energy source for the future called *nuclear fusion*.

Nuclear energy comes from the nucleus of an atom. The kind of nuclear energy that we use now comes from *nuclear fission*. Fission is the process of splitting atoms apart. Fusion is the process of joining atoms together. When either process happens, a huge amount of energy is released. In nuclear fission, atoms are split apart by firing a single small nucleus into a mass of large nuclei. In nuclear fusion, the nuclei of hydrogen atoms are heated to very high temperatures. The heat makes the nuclei move around very fast. As they move faster and faster, they bump into each other at such a speed that they join together, or fuse. A lot of energy is released when the nuclei fuse.

The Mimi sure looked different with a coat of snow.

Fusion is the energy process that happens on the sun. The scientists at M.I.T. are trying to recreate the environment of the sun. This means that they have to heat up the hydrogen gas to tremendously high temperatures. At such temperatures a gas is called a plasma. In the machine, or fusion reactor, that Peter is working on, the plasma becomes hotter than the sun. It reaches a temperature of 70 million degrees Celsius.

"Seventy million degrees?" cried Ben. "Peter, there's no way the gas in this machine could get hotter than the sun. Everything would melt. This whole building would melt." Peter explained that that's where magnets come in. The superhot plasma never touches the walls of the machine. It is contained in a small area and held there by large electromagnets. The magnetic field is a force strong enough to hold the plasma in a small area. Peter says that the fusion reactor is like a giant bottle whose walls are a magnetic field.

Ben thought it was pretty amazing that magnetic force can do so many things. It can contain the power of the sun, or help sailors and explorers to navigate. It can also be a lot of fun for kids to play with.

Electromagnets are more powerful than permanent magnets. The small electromagnet, shown in the photo below, was stronger than Ben. Some big ones, shown on the right, can hold a gas that's even hotter than the sun.

Try this. You'll need a bar magnet with the poles marked (N and S) and a pocket compass with the colored end of the needle pointing north.

1. Bring the S-pole of the bar magnet near the compass. What happened? What conclusion can you draw about *unlike* poles?
2. Now turn the bar magnet around so the N-pole is near the compass. What happened? What conclusion can you draw about *like* poles?

But wait a minute! Remember the question Ben asked Peter? If like poles repel, why does the *north* end of a compass needle point to the earth's *north* pole? Do you remember Peter's explanation? If you don't remember, can you think of a way to explain this puzzling fact?

GLOSSARY

adaptation: a change that makes an organism better able to survive in its environment

alchemist: a person who tries to use magical power to change something of little value into something precious

altimeter: a device used to measure distance above sea level or above the earth's surface

aquifer: an underground water supply

artifact: an object made by a human being to be used for a specific purpose

atmosphere: the air; the major part of an environment

atmospheric pressure: a measure of the pressure of the atmosphere pushing on the earth

audiology: the science of hearing

automatic direction finder (ADF): a device that indicates the direction to the source of a transmitted signal

baleen: a material that grows from the upper jaws of certain whales, used to filter food from water (see humpback whale illustration, p. 6)

bank: a broad area where the sea floor rises so that the water is more shallow than in other areas

barnacle: a small marine animal with a shell that attaches itself to rocks, ships, and even slow-moving ocean creatures

barometer: an instrument for measuring atmospheric pressure, which is used to predict weather changes

bearing: the direction or position of an object, usually measured in degrees on a compass

belay: in sailing, to secure a rope by winding it around a pin or short post

binnacle: a stand that holds a boat's or ship's compass

block and tackle: a device for lifting that uses pulleys and ropes or chains

bow: the front part of a boat or ship (see *Mimi* illustration, p. 4)

bowsprit: a wooden or metal pole pointing forward from the bow of a boat or ship that holds the rigging of sails (see *Mimi* illustration, p. 4)

Braille: a system of writing for the blind made up of dots or points to represent letters and numbers to be read by touch; named after Louis Braille, who invented it

breach: a behavior of the humpback whale in which the whale leaps almost completely out of the water

callosities: tough, wartlike growths on the heads of right whales

caulk: to seal or close up a seam or joint of a boat

census: a procedure for counting a population and describing its members

channel: a part of a waterway that is deeper than the areas on either side of it

characteristic: the behavior and appearance of a person or thing that make it different from others

companionway: a stairway or ladder inside a boat

compass: an instrument with a magnetic needle for finding directions

compost: a mixture of decayed organic matter, such as dead leaves or manure, used for fertilizing land

condensation: the process by which a gas or a vapor, such as steam, cools and is reduced to a liquid form

contour line: a line on a map connecting places that have the same height or depth

core temperature: the temperature of the central, most important part of a body

crosstrees: a platform near the top of a mast on a sailing boat or ship; the crow's nest (see *Mimi* illustration, p. 4)

crow's nest: a platform used as a lookout near the top of a mast on a sailing vessel; crosstrees (see *Mimi* illustration, p. 4)

D

dehydration: the removal or loss of water or moisture, especially from the body

denticle: a small tooth

dividers: an instrument used to divide or measure lines

dorsal fin: a fin on the back (dorsal side) of a sea creature, such as a whale (see humpback whale illustration, p. 6)

dory: a small boat with a narrow, flat bottom

E

echo sounder: an instrument that calculates water depth by sending sound pulses down to the ocean floor and measuring the time it takes the echo to return

echolocation: a way of locating objects by sending out sound waves and using the returning echo to determine distance, shape, and size

electromagnet: a magnet made by surrounding an iron or steel core by a coil through which electricity flows

endangered: threatened; in danger of becoming extinct

environment: a combination of all the conditions that affect how a person or thing exists and grows

evaporation: the process in which moisture is heated and turns to a gas (vapor)

evolution: the process of gradual change by which organisms adapt to their environment

expendable bathythermograph (XBT): a device used to measure ocean temperatures at different depths; a sensor falls through the water at a constant rate and reports the temperatures at regular intervals; called expendable because the sensor is used only once

extinction: the process of dying out, ceasing to exist

extremities: the ends of arms and legs; the parts of the body furthest from the heart

F

fathom: a unit of measurement equal to 6 feet, used to indicate water depth

flukes: the flat part at the end of a whale's tail

fo'c'sle (forecastle): the most forward part of a boat or ship below deck, used as sleeping quarters or for storage (see *Mimi* illustration, p. 4)

food chain: a number of organisms dependent upon one another for their food needs, with one organism eating another and being eaten in turn by still another

fossil: the remains or evidence, such as a skeleton or footprint, of an animal or plant from an earlier time on earth

furling line: a rope used to hold a rolled-up or gathered sail when the sail is not in use

fuse: a protective device, used in an electric circuit; when too much current flows through a piece of metal in the fuse, the metal melts and stops the flow of electricity

G

galley: the kitchen area of a vessel

geophysicist: a scientist who specializes in matter and energy in relation to the earth

glucose: a sugar found in many fruits and in animal tissues

gunnel (gunwale): the upper part of the hull of a boat

H

halyard: a rope used to raise and lower a sail (see *Mimi* illustration, p. 4)

hatch (hatchway): a covered opening in the deck of a boat or ship

heading: the compass direction in which a vessel is traveling; course

hydrophone: a device used to find the source of underwater sounds

hypothermia: the condition of a body when it loses so much heat that the core temperature drops below normal

I

insulation: wrapping, covering, or in some other way protecting something from losing heat

intersect: to cross; to divide by passing through or across

J

jib: a triangular sail (see *Mimi* illustration, p. 4)

K

knot: a unit of speed that equals one nautical mile per hour

knotmeter: an instrument that measures the speed in knots of a boat or ship

krill: small, shrimplike marine creatures used as food by some kinds of whales

L

latitude: distance north or south from the equator on the earth's surface, measured in degrees

lead line: a rope marked off in fathoms and having a weight on the end, used to measure water depth

lobtail: a behavior of humpback whales; with its head pointing down in the water, the whale sticks its tail out of the water and slaps its flukes against the water surface

longitude: distance east or west on the earth's surface, measured in degrees

M

mainsail: the lowermost sail on the mainmast (see *Mimi* illustration, p. 4)

mammal: a vertebrate (an animal having a spinal column) that nurses its young, has hair on its body, and gives birth to live babies

mammalogist: a scientist who specializes in mammals

marine biologist: a scientist who specializes in animals and plants that live in the ocean

marine geologist: a scientist who specializes in the history and physical features of the parts of the earth that are or once were under the sea

mass: a measure that combines the weight, size, and density of an object

mast: a tall, polelike structure that holds the sails and rigging on a boat (see *Mimi* illustration, p. 4)

meteorologist: a scientist who specializes in weather and climate

microalgae: tiny plants that can be seen only through a microscope

microwave: an electromagnetic wave that can be sent over long distances

mizzen: a sail on the mizzenmast, the shorter mast on a boat like the *Mimi* (see *Mimi* illustration, p. 4)

molecule: the smallest physical part of something, composed of atoms and too small to be seen without special equipment such as a microscope

multimeter: a device used to measure electrical voltage, which causes electric current to flow

mysticete: a whale that has baleen (instead of teeth)

N

nuclear fission: the splitting apart of the nucleus of an atom, resulting in the release of energy

nuclear fusion: the joining together (fusing) of the nuclei of atoms

O

oceanographer: a scientist who studies the physical characteristics of the earth's oceans

odontocete: a whale that has teeth (instead of baleen)

P

parrel beads: strand of round, wooden beads used to hoist a sail smoothly up the mast

physicist: a scientists who specializes in matter and energy

pitch: 1) the highness or lowness of a tone or sound; 2) a dark, sticky substance used to seal wood or other material against water and weather

plankton: small organisms that float and drift in water

plasma: a gas so hot that its molecules have broken into elementary particles

plateau: an area of fairly level land that is higher than the surrounding area

pod: a herd or group of whales or other animals

port: the left-hand side of a vessel, facing forward (see *Mimi* illustration, p. 4)

precipitation: rain, snow, hail, sleet; what falls from the sky as a result of condensation

proboscis: a long snout or beak

profile: an outlined side view of something

prow: the front of a vessel; the bow

psychologist: a scientist who specializes in the human mind and behavior

R

radio direction finder (RDF): an instrument used in navigation to help figure out location; the RDF antenna receives radio signals that allow navigators to get bearings to radio stations whose location they know and to use those bearings to figure out their position

receiver: a device such as a radio, telephone, or television set that receives signals and makes them understandable

reservoir: a place where water is collected and stored

rigging: the ropes, chains, and other equipment that support the masts, sails, and other parts of a vessel and make them work

rime ice: tiny ice particles caused by the rapid freezing of water droplets when they touch a cold object

rostrum: the flat, front part of the top of a whale's head (see humpback whale illustration, p. 6)

S

salinity meter: an instrument that measures the salt content of liquids

saloon: a large cabin for general use by the people on a boat or ship

sector: a smaller division of a larger area, set off by lines or boundaries

shoals: an area of the ocean that is very shallow

short circuit: a condition that causes too much electricity to flow, leading to overheating

sloop: a kind of sailboat with only one mast

solar still: a device for using the sun's energy to purify water by means of evaporation and condensation

soundings: measurements of water depth, usually obtained by using an echo sounder

species: the basic category used for classifying living things that have certain characteristics in common

specimen: a typical example of something (species) such as a plant or animal

spectrogram: a drawing or photograph of patterns produced by sounds played into a spectrum analyzer

spectrum analyzer: a machine that analyzes sound and produces a visual image so that the patterns in the sound can be seen and studied

starboard: the right-hand side of a vessel, facing forward (see *Mimi* illustration, p. 4)

staysail: a sail set on a rope (see *Mimi* illustration, p. 4)

stern: the back part of a boat (see *Mimi* illustration, p. 4)

T

thermistor: an electronic device for measuring temperature

thermophysicist: a scientist who specializes in how temperature affects matter and energy

thermoregulation: the way living creatures respond to temperature changes and maintain their body temperatures

tidepool: a pool of water left after the tide has gone out, often containing a variety of sea life

tilapia: a hardy tropical fish well-suited for fish farming

transect: to cut across; a line or path that crosses a specific area

transmitter: a device for sending out communication signals

tropopause: the boundary between two layers of the earth's atmosphere

tubercle: a small round bump on the face of the bodies of some animals (see p. 6)

V

vapor: an element that has been changed to a gas and mixed with air

ventral pleats: grooves in the skin on the underside of some whales allowing the whale's body to expand as it feeds (see humpback whale illustration, p. 6)

vertebrate paleontologist: a scientist who specializes in the fossils of animals with backbones

W

whisker stay: a wire or chain running from the tip of the bowsprit to the port and starboard sides of the bow to provide support for the bowsprit (see *Mimi* illustration, p. 4)

winch: a device with a crank used for lifting and hauling

wind chill: the effect of wind in creating a sensation of lower temperature

Acknowledgments

The quality of the content and design of this book owes much to the talented and skillful people at Holt, Rinehart and Winston School Publishing who worked heroically under impossible deadlines on all the "Mimi" print materials. In particular, we wish to thank Eileen Mitchell, whose intelligent and careful editing and refreshing good cheer never yielded to the constant pressures of time (too little) and volume (too much); Carol Steinberg and the Design staff, particularly Arlene Kosarin Morelli, Margo Hrubec, Marta Ruliffson and Randi Wasserman for capturing the spirit of the project in design and art; Joan McNeil for skillful production; and Dorothy Shao and Karen Gotimer for gentle, wise, and effective editorial supervision.

ART CREDITS

Skip Sorvino – Cover design
Sal Catalano – Cover art
Wayne Mcloughlin – The Mimi
  p. 4–5
Richard Ellis – Humpback Whale
  p. 6–7

Episode Art

Simon Galkin
  Episode 5
Michael Garland
  Episodes 1,6,8,10,13
Alex Gnidziejko
  Episode 2
Alan Reingold
  Episodes 4,7,12
Jon Weiman
  Episodes 3,9,11

Activity Art

Kimble Mead – p. 12, p. 27
Min Jae Hong – p. 13, p. 93
Sal Murdocca – p. 39, p. 81,
  p. 140–141
Randi Wasserman – p. 49, p. 70–71
Cynthia Watts Clark – p. 59,
  p. 117, p. 127
David Palladini – p. 104–105
Bradley Hales Clark – p. 150–151

PHOTO CREDITS

All photographs by Martha Cooper for Holt, Rinehart and Winston except:
top: Richard Kolar/Animals, Animals, Inc.; Allan Morgan/ Peter Arnold, Inc.; p. 29
top left: William Curtsinger/Photo Researchers, Inc.; top right: Eda Rogers '83; bottom: Russ Kinne/ Photo Researchers, Inc.; p. 30
top: F. Gohier, 1982/Photo Researchers, Inc.; bottom: Russ Kinne/Photo Researchers, Inc.; p. 31
Anita Brosius; p. 40-42
Mark J. Ferrari; p. 74
Richard Hendrick; p. 94-97
Barbara Kirk for Holt, Rinehart and Winston; p. 152-155

Whaling journal excerpt (Episode 4, p. 48):
  From *One Whaling Family,* edited by Harold Williams, published by Houghton Mifflin Company. Copyright © 1964 by Houghton Mifflin Company. Reprinted by permission of the publisher.

Poem ("A baby whale is come . . . ") (Episode 6 activities, p. 71):
  From *There's a Sound in the Sea: A Child's-Eye View of the Whale,* collected by Tamar Griggs, published by The Scrimshaw Press. Copyright © 1975 by Tamar Griggs. Reprinted by permission of Tamar Griggs.

Quote by Jacques-Yves Cousteau: (Expedition 1, p. 16):
  From "The Ocean: A Perspective," *National Geographic,* vol. 160, no. 6 (December, 1981) pp. 781–782. Copyright © 1981, National Geographic Society. Reprinted by permission.